AFFAIRS OF
THE HEART
SECOND EDITION

Book One of the Sisters Trilogy
Affairs of the Heart Universe

MiChele Mitchell

Affairs of the Heart Universe

A generational saga of love,
loyalty, sisterhood, marriage,
and the quiet work of becoming whole.

Every wedding is a beginning.
Every family carries history.
Every heart keeps secrets.

All stories are connected.

Continue the Journey

Sisters Trilogy

Affairs of the Heart

Unbreakable

Truth & Love

DEDICATION

To those who

are still in search of *The One*.

ACKNOWLEDGMENTS

First and foremost, I want to thank God, through Him all things are possible. Thank you to my parents for always wanting great things for me and for encouraging me to be my absolute best. Gwendolyn Parish, my big sister, thank you for all your encouragement and support throughout my life and throughout my book writing process. But most of all, thank you for loving me and praying for me when I needed it the most. Kimberly Gooden, thank you for being my bestie, my biggest cheerleader and for showing me by example that all you have to do to get the story out of your head and into a book is to just do it. Marilyn Barriera, thank you for all your help. Saudia Twine, my little sister, thank you for taking time during your studies to assist me with this book. I am so thankful to be related to one of the few other 1%ers in the world. You understand me and the way I think like no one else can. Kevin Parish, I know that we joke a lot, but I love you and I appreciate your help. Thank you for being good to my sister and for always being my reminder that good guys do exist. Joyce Mitchell and Bobbie Hayes-Goodrum, thank you both for your editing skills. I appreciate you more than you'll ever know. Summer Scarbough, thank you for believing in me and for reminding me not to take life too seriously. Angelique Gholston Harris, you may not even know when you did it, but you gave me the idea to write this book. Thank you!

I have such wonderful children... My sons, Tre' and Mitchell, thank you for your support and for sharing your time with me so that I could write this book. My daughter, Alyssa, thank you for constantly checking to make sure that I was working on the book when I was supposed to be and for making sure that I met my deadlines. Gwen, Kimber and Marilyn thank you again for the countless hours spent in the trenches with me from beginning to end. I couldn't have done it without you. Thank You, Thank You, Thank You! I love you all... May peace be upon you. ~Cinco5five

PROLOGUE

My name is Julianna. My family and close friends call me Jewels. I, along with my sisters, Lisa and India, have an event planning company and we specialize in weddings. I am a wedding planner. Most women spend their whole lives dreaming of their wedding day, and it's my job to make that dream come true. Our company, Affairs of the Heart, has a slogan, *Happily Ever After… Begins with Us!* and it is so true. Happily Ever After does begin on the wedding day. That I can guarantee. The cold reality is that there is no real guarantee that it will last. It's all based on this thing called love. What is love? Does anyone really know? We know a mother's love, the love you have for your siblings and your friends. What about love for a significant other? Is it like we see on television or like we hear in the love songs? Who really knows—Google, Dr. Phil, Steve Harvey, or Luther Vandross? Google says that love is an intense feeling of deep affection. Dr. Phil says that you have to love smart by loving yourself first. Steve Harvey says that you have to act like a lady and think like a man. And Luther told us that *It's So Amazing*, it's *Here and Now*, *Love Won't Let Me Wait* and it's *Always and Forever*. Hmm, all those definitions sound good to me. I used to think that there was only one true love for each of us. I thought that if you really loved someone, they MUST be The One.

The truth of the matter is that while I can put together a fabulous wedding, I don't know any more than anyone else when it comes to understanding love. My quest for love has been rough, to say the least. It took me a long time to figure out who was the right one for me. I dated in high school, but my search really began at my sister's wedding.

PART ONE:
Life

Chapter 1
The Wedding Planner

Walking through the front doors of the church, you were immediately met by the soft scents of Asiatic lilies, roses, and eucalyptus. The air conditioning was a welcome relief from the August heat. The bride sat in her fluffy white wedding gown staring up at the ceiling as a makeup artist in a black fitted top and black pants reached into the tool belt strapped around her waist for the proper brush to touch up the bride's face before she walked down the aisle. The big day had finally arrived. Lisa Jeffries was getting married.

At 22, Lisa was marrying Michael Daniels. Everyone expected this day to come as Lisa and Michael were high school sweethearts. They were voted class couple at Mumford High School and were together all the time. Their life seemed to be like the stories you see on television. For some reason Lisa didn't like it when people said that her life was perfect, but from the outside looking in, it did seem that way. They had their differences, as all couples do, but in the grand scheme of things, life was pretty good.

Lisa had spent a year working with her wedding planner to set all the details of her wedding. Her wedding planner, Julianna Jeffries, was Lisa's younger sister. Julianna and Lisa had eight years of experience working in their aunt's flower shop decorating for weddings. Julianna had always been a thorough researcher. She studied weddings and had the knowledge to make everything Lisa envisioned happen. Some people may have found it odd that Lisa had a 19-year-old for a wedding planner. However, Lisa and Julianna were close and very much alike, so Lisa was confident that Julianna would execute the wedding to her satisfaction. Julianna asked two of her friends, Carmen and William, to help her.

Carmen placed corsages on the wrists of both mothers and all the hostesses. She also pinned boutonnières on both fathers and all of the ushers. Julianna took care of the wedding party. She paid special attention to her 16-year-old sister India and Michael's younger sister Gabriella, who were bridesmaids and her 10-year-old brother Jonathan who was the ring bearer. Julianna did a final check on India and Gabriella's dresses and hair. She wanted to review with them and the other bridesmaids—one last time—the proper way to carry a bouquet. Before she left the room, she tested Jonathan and the flower girl to make sure that they remembered what they were supposed to do. As the guests began to arrive, William made sure that they all received programs and were seated.

Julianna entered the pastor's study where the groom and groomsmen were waiting. She noticed the best man who was Michael's best friend, Anthony Franklin. As

Julianna pinned the boutonnière on Anthony's lapel, she realized that while she had seen him before, it was as though she was seeing him for the first time. All the sounds in the room went dim, and everything seemed to be moving in slow motion as Julianna secretly looked him up and down. Anthony was tall with a muscular build. His warm complexion was a striking contrast to his dark eyes and coal black wavy hair. Julianna had a thing for nice mouths, and he had one. He had straight, white teeth and nice pink lips that were beautifully accented with a finely trimmed mustache. To top everything off, he smelled wonderful. Julianna recognized his cologne—it was Lagerfeld. Maybe it was the tuxedo, or maybe it was the fact that he seemed to have been seriously working out, but Mr. Franklin did not look like that before. He was definitely looking good.

Julianna cued the music and Kenny G's version of Songbird played as the line of pink dresses and black tuxedos proceeded to the front of the church. Julianna left the sanctuary to do a final check on Lisa. Two ushers walked together to the front of the church, reached down and pulled the white lace runner to the back of the church before the flower girl covered it with pink rose petals. The music changed to Mendelssohn's *Wedding March*, and the audience stood while Carmen and William opened the sanctuary doors. Lisa and her father were standing in the doorway. Julianna carried the back of Lisa's dress and gently laid it on the floor after Lisa cleared the doorway. The ear-to-ear smile on Michael's face when he saw Lisa was a clear sign that he could see how beautiful she was from all the way at the front of the church.

Endless Love by Diana Ross and Lionel Richie played as the new Mr. and Mrs. Michael Daniels entered the ballroom for their reception. They had their first dance as husband and wife just before they cut their wedding cake. Shortly after the wedding party and guests completed their meal, all the single ladies were called to the dance floor for the bouquet toss. Gabriella and Julianna were standing next to each other. The moment Lisa threw her bouquet, Julianna saw it coming her way. It landed right in her hands. Lisa was asked to sit in the chair that William placed in the center of the room. Michael kneeled before her, reached under her dress and removed her garter without showing the least bit of Lisa's leg to the guests. The single men were then called to the dance floor for the garter toss. Anthony caught the garter.

The DJ played *I Feel for You* by Chaka Khan and opened the dance floor to all the guests. Julianna's debut wedding was just a couple of hours away from coming to a successful close. She, Carmen, and William sat down to rest. She was pleased with the day and how everything went, but she was daydreaming about going home and falling into her bed. Just as she thought that she had done everything that there was to do for everyone who needed anything done, Anthony approached her and said that he had a request. He extended his hand and asked Julianna to dance.

Carmen noticed Julianna look around for Lisa and Michael to make sure that they were okay. "Don't worry; I'll take care of them."

Julianna smiled at Carmen, then turned back and placed her hand in Anthony's, and they danced… for the rest of the night.

Chapter 2
Carmen Perez

Julianna...

The summer after I turned eight, my family left the suburban world of Taylor, Michigan, and moved back to Detroit—the city where my parents were born and raised. Our new house sat on Abington, just off Schoolcraft. I didn't know it then, but that move would shape everything.

The first person I met was the girl who lived directly across the street—Carmen Perez. She was nine and already seemed like she owned the block. She had an older brother, Hector, and a family story that felt bigger than mine. They had moved to Michigan from Puerto Rico after her dad's job transferred him. Her mother stayed home, was always cooking something that smelled incredible, and spoke almost completely in Spanish. I didn't understand most of what she said back then, but I loved the sound of it.

Carmen and I sat on the porch that first day, our legs swinging, and she told me about everyone on the block—who fought, who lied, who thought they were cute, who actually was. While we were sitting there, a boy walked out of the house next door to mine. Carmen leaned in like she was sharing classified information and told me his name was Christopher. He had an older brother and a younger sister. She introduced me to him that same afternoon, along with everyone else who mattered.

From that day on, Carmen and I went to the same schools and became inseparable. You couldn't be friends with Carmen and have low self-esteem. It just wasn't possible. She turned heads without trying. By sixteen, she was five-foot-five with a perfectly proportioned body and long curly brown hair that she worked hard to keep straight. Her skin always looked toasted—like she had just stepped off a Puerto Rican beach—and her face was effortlessly beautiful.

But what made Carmen unforgettable wasn't her looks. It was her spirit. She was carefree, warm, inviting. Being around her felt like sunlight.

By the time we graduated high school, she had me speaking fluent Spanish. We used it to have private conversations in plain sight, saying exactly what we wanted while everyone else smiled and nodded. We talked about everything.

But my favorite subject?

Christopher.

PART TWO:

In Like

Chapter 3
Christopher Charles

Julianna...

Christopher Charles was my next-door neighbor, my friend, and my first love. Throughout our childhood, we talked, played together, and became close. There were several other kids on the block, and we all hung out together, but Christopher and I were inseparable. Once puberty kicked in, the dynamic between us began to change. We found ourselves attracted to each other in a different way. Christopher's complexion was naturally light, but because we were outside so much, he always had a tan. He had big brown eyes and soft curly hair.

Our favorite game was hide-'n-seek. Okay, that's the game the other kids were playing. Christopher and I were playing our version of hide-'n-go-get'em. We would always hide together and spend the time making out while everyone else was running around looking for us.

I was allowed to have company, but only when my parents were home. When they were at work, I could go outside, but only on the porch. Christopher, however, came to the house regularly in the absence of my parents. One day, while my parents were at work, Christopher and I were in the basement playing pool. When I went upstairs, I heard the phone ring. It rang twice, then it stopped. I went back downstairs only to realize that it stopped ringing because Christopher had answered it; he said that it was my father who had called and that he wanted me to call him back. Panic quickly set in while I frantically tried to think of a way to explain how Christopher could have answered the phone without being in the house.

An idea hit me. When I called him, I told my father that I was sitting on the front porch with Christopher, so I took the phone out there with me. It was still sitting on the porch when I went in the house for a minute, and he answered it when it rang. Whew! I dodged that bullet. Looking back, knowing my father the way I did, I realized that he probably knew the truth, and just gave me credit for coming up with a good cover story.

Every summer for six years it was the same; Christopher, me, and everyone else hanging out and kickin' it, having fun, and getting in trouble together. Every year Christopher and I got closer and went a little bit further. We got older, and hormones were raging. The summer after I turned 14 was the most sexually intense for us. I had always loved Christopher and was ready to have sex with him, but I was nervous. By the end of the summer, we had a day where all the planets aligned—except one. No one was home at my house. We were in the den making out. I wanted to have sex; he definitely wanted to. The one problem was that it was that time of the month. I figured that it was no big deal; we would just have to wait until next time.

The following January Christopher turned 16 and got his driver's license. For his birthday, he got a candy apple red Mustang. Needless to say, his dating options were no longer limited to the block or the girl next door. In the spring of the following year, my family moved to a more affluent neighborhood called the University District on Parkside Street. Christopher and I always remained friends, but that was the end of that.

I was talking to and spending time with a boy that I went to school with, but Christopher was my first intimate experience, although despite popular belief, we never actually had sex.

Chapter 4
Dean Lawson

Julianna...

The gym was on the second floor at school, and the weight room was attached to it. The head football coach had his players lifting weights. I was working the snack table in the weight room doorway, selling candy to raise money for the Athletic Department. Dean was a senior transfer student and track and football star who came to Cooley High—well-known for its athletics—because he needed to be at a school where he could get scouted for college. He was 5'11" and had the most beautiful shade of chocolate brown skin. He was wearing a t-shirt and shorts that left his arms and legs exposed and every muscle he had was very well defined. He had brown eyes and short black hair with deep brush waves. His full set of bright, shiny braces didn't take away from his smile, and his dimples just made him even more good-looking.

After Dean had been at the table for a minute, I said, "Well hey, you can't speak?"

Dean said, "I spoke to you when I saw you earlier. Am I supposed to speak to you every time I see you?"

"Yes," I said.

"Well, what am I supposed to do on the weekends?"

"Pick up the phone, dial 273-4359, ask to speak to me and then say hello."

"Oh okay, I'll remember that." And he went back into the weight room to finish his workout.

That night, Lisa, India, and I were in the kitchen with our mother when the phone rang. Lisa was standing right next to the phone, which was hanging on the wall, so she picked it up and said, "Hello?—Who's calling?—

Hold on just a minute." Lisa held the phone out and said, "Jewels, it's for you."

I reached for the phone and said, "Thanks, who is it?"

Lisa said, "It's Dean."

I snatched my hand back and held it to my chest and whispered, "What? Stop playing with me, who is it?"

Lisa laughed and said, "I told you, it's Dean."

In a quiet scream, I said, "Oh my God! Big, fine, hot as they come—he's a senior and I'm a freshman—Dean is calling me. He didn't even write the number down. He remembered it all that time. Oh, my God!"

Lisa and our mother looked at each other and laughed. Lisa said, "So do you want to talk to him or not?"

"Yes! Okay, yes… I want to talk to him; would you hang up the phone when I get in my room?"

On my way up the stairs, I could hear Lisa say, "She'll be right with you." Then I heard more laughter.

I regained my composure, went into my room, and picked up the telephone. I could hardly believe that I was talking to him.

Dean had recently broken up with one of the most popular girls in school. She was a cheerleader and a senior whose friends were not happy when Dean and I were seen in school together, especially when we were seen leaving school together. I was public enemy number one, but it was so worth it. Dean was a really sweet guy. We fell asleep talking on the phone every night and saw each other in school each day. We went to his house and hung out, but he never pressured me about sex. He said if I wasn't ready, it was alright, he just wanted to spend time with me. It worked out really well because even though I thought I was ready with Christopher, I wasn't ready to go there with anyone else.

Dean received a full football scholarship to the University of Notre Dame. He wasn't just a jock, he was also very intelligent. At the end of the school year, he went straight to college. He didn't hang out for the summer. He didn't even wait for his graduation ceremony. He hated being in Detroit and couldn't wait to leave. Even though Dean said that I shouldn't, I took it personally. I couldn't believe that he walked away from me so easily. I thought that he would wait until the very last minute to leave. My concern was that I would never see him again. He said that we would talk and that he would visit, but it didn't clear up that knot in my stomach. I didn't see him at all that summer. The times that I wasn't with my sisters, I spent with Carmen. That fall, when school started, Dean began coming home for visits, and William entered my life.

PART THREE:

Love

Chapter 5
Nigel William Nicholson IV

Julianna...

I met Mr. Nigel William Nicholson IV during a test in our accounting class. I looked to my right, and he was leaning over looking at my paper. I would never say he copied off my work... I wouldn't say it, but he did. We were friends from that day on. He became a part of my family, and I became a part of his. We were together so much that we had to tell people that we were brother and sister because people couldn't wrap their minds around the fact that a guy and a girl could just be friends. We went from just friends to the best of friends our senior year in high school.

He was the fourth generation of Nigels, so his family called him William. William and Carmen hit it off as well, which made life easy for me, so I didn't have to choose between them. I could hang out with both of them at the same time if that's how it worked out. Actually, I was sure that William had a crush on Carmen. He always asked about her when she wasn't around and would just kind of space out, shake his head and say the only thing he knew in Spanish, "Una señorita es muy caliente!" (That girl is very hot!)—or at least, that's what he was trying to say.

William stood about six feet three inches tall—a huge stretch from the five feet six inches he was our sophomore and junior years of high school. Oh, what a difference a year made. He grew up into quite a handsome man. Chocolate and slim, with a minimum of three layers of designer clothing, and the biggest, brightest smile around. He was funny, extremely charming, and a complete gentleman. William spoiled me throughout the years of our friendship. He never forgot a birthday or a holiday, and he picked out cards so perfect that if I didn't know better, I would have thought that he had the people at Hallmark write them especially for me.

It seemed that William treated the women he dated at least as well, but he went through women so quickly that he and I rarely spoke in detail about any of them. He wanted me to meet his new girlfriend, Autumn. He said that she wasn't the same as the rest of his girlfriends—and she wasn't. She ended up having a major effect on my life.

Chapter 6
Autumn Goodwin

Julianna…

After school one Friday, I was heading to the parking lot with Dean—who was in town for a visit—when I saw William's Bronco blocking my car. William was leaning up against his truck with a girl whom I assumed to be Autumn, his latest and greatest. Autumn Goodwin attended a predominantly white private all-girls school, Mercy High, in Farmington Hills. William went through girls rather quickly so I would hear him, but rarely listened, when he talked about them. I hadn't thought much about Autumn prior to this initial encounter, but she wasn't at all what I expected. Autumn was beautiful, as were all of William's girls, but there was something different about her. Her skin had a glow that looked as if she had permanent bronzer applied. Her hair was straight and pulled back into a ponytail. Her eyebrows were perfectly arched, and she had on just enough makeup to complement her natural beauty. Her breasts were small but suited her frame perfectly, paired with a tiny waist and shapely hips. She looked all prim and proper in her Roman Catholic school uniform. Although she did a pretty good job of disguising it, her attitude was slightly "hood".

During Dean's visits home, he and I double dated with William and Autumn a few times before Autumn, and I started becoming friends. As I got to know Autumn better, I found out where that "hood" thing came from. Autumn lived off Livernois and Puritan and her brother Craig was paying her tuition with drug money. Autumn and Craig seemed to function together, when necessary, but I thought the relationship was fairly superficial because it didn't seem as though they actually liked each other too much. Although they were both good-looking people, they didn't look alike apart from their hazel eyes. Autumn always had money and dressed very well when she wasn't in uniform. I jokingly called her Dynasty because she looked like one of those rich Carringtons from the old television show Dynasty.

Autumn was a very touchy-feely type of person. I had met people like that before but somehow it was different with Autumn. She never did anything that I could point out and say for certain that Autumn was gay—it was just a feeling that I got. Autumn always touched me just a little too often and would hold the touch just a little too long. It didn't matter to me if Autumn was gay or not; I just wondered why Autumn wouldn't tell me. She was dating William, so maybe she wasn't ready to admit it to herself.

As with all of William's girls, his relationship with Autumn was short-lived, but by then Autumn and I were already good friends. While it did get tricky from time to time because it seemed to take Autumn a little longer to get over it, I was able to maintain my friendship with both William and Autumn. I spent a lot of time with Autumn.

Autumn invited me to a lobster boil at her brother Craig's house. Although Craig still sold drugs in the neighborhood where they grew up, he no longer lived there. Craig lived a high-class life that left people shocked when they found out what he did for a living.

There were friends and family at the house and that was the first time I saw live lobsters being dropped into boiling water. I found it pretty normal when Autumn introduced me to Craig's wife, but things instantly got more interesting five minutes later when Autumn introduced me to Craig's girlfriend. Yup, everybody hanging out in the house together, getting along just fine. Who knew people actually lived that way? I felt like if it worked for them, who was I to judge. We all had a great time and that was all that mattered to me.

A few months later, Autumn and I were out shopping at Fairlane Mall in Dearborn when Autumn asked me if I minded if we made a stop on the way back. I was fine with it, so we went down the street to the Residence Inn. We parked and went up to Room 225 and knocked on the door. Autumn's brother Craig stood behind the door—as he opened it. When we entered, we could see that he had an Uzi in his hand. I wasn't afraid of guns—not really—but I didn't understand why he was walking around with one. Whatever business Autumn had with him was quick because we were in and out. Autumn explained that Craig was on the run; he was on Michigan's Most Wanted List for murder. Craig didn't seem like a killer to me, but I actually had no clue as to what a killer would seem like. When we left, Autumn said that she should turn Craig in for the reward money. When I looked at her, Autumn laughed. It seemed like what India called "cracking but facking"—saying something true but playing it off like a joke. I wasn't sure how I felt about the Most Wanted thing, but I was sure that I didn't want any part of it.

Chapter 7
Jewels by Autumn

Autumn...

I've seen a lot during my lifetime. I know that my brother Craig made a better future possible for me. It definitely wasn't the most traditional route, but it got me where I am today. All my classmates lived in neighborhoods like Jewels' and William's. I rarely told anyone exactly where I lived because I'd had enough of people looking down on me and judging me. My life was put together for me by me (with Craig's assistance) and I didn't feel as though I owed anyone any explanations as to how I made it happen.

Befriending (and later dating) William was like a breath of fresh air. He was nothing like the guys that I grew up with. He was sweet, nonviolent, a gentleman. His parents were married and had money. He talked a mile a minute, had an infectious laugh, and was loyal to a fault. He took great pleasure in his appearance, and he was quite easy on the eyes. That smile so white that it rivaled the best that Hollywood had to offer. We didn't last long on the dating scene, but we remained friends. William always talked about his best friend, Jewels. He would tell me how they raced each other from their neighborhood to Belle Isle every chance they got. He knew that I didn't have many close friends, but he thought that she and I would hit it off. Again, I was very guarded about my home situation at the time, but William did have me curious about meeting Jewels.

One evening he was, yet again, talking about racing Jewels. This time, she beat him to the freeway but once he got there, he caught up to her and effortlessly passed her. I asked him, "If you two are so close, why haven't I met her yet?" I'm all for friends of the opposite sex, but if he's my man, I should at least know her. He said that next time they were hanging out he'd let me know.

Later that week, William told me that he would pick me up outside of school. We drove to Cooley High School on Fenkell and Hubbell, pulled into the student parking lot and parked behind a red Mazda 323. We were leaning against the front of his Bronco when William pointed Jewels out to me. She was walking across the parking lot accompanied by a handsome brother who William revealed was Dean Lawson. He was carrying her backpack for her as they talked and laughed. She was wearing a form fitting red t-shirt with a cardinal and black writing that read Cooley Class of 1986. The shirt highlighted her full breasts and small waist. Her denim jeans seemed painted on her round full hips and lengthy legs.

Her hair was long, dark, and thick. It was a texture that only required a brush and some water to control. As I watched her talking animatedly, I couldn't help but hear her ultra-feminine voice. Topping that off was a delightful, attractive face. She had large brown eyes, long eyelashes, naturally arched eyebrows, and full organically pink lips all set on skin the color of a caramel apple. Even in her red low top Nikes with the black swoosh, she walked with a natural rhythm that somehow seemed to sway her hips. You could tell that she held a natural grace. As she gestured to Dean, her wrist was arched in an unusual, incredibly ladylike way.

She introduced herself as Julianna. All that time, William had me thinking that girl's name was Jewels. Oh well, she was Jewels to him, so now she's Jewels to me. There was something about that initial meeting that made me know that we were destined to become friends. She introduced me to Dean, kissed him, and told him that she would see him later.

Chapter 8
Guess Who's Coming to Dinner

Lisa's bridal shower was outside on a hot, sunny July afternoon. There were white tables, chairs, and tents. All her bridesmaids came together to give her an unforgettable day. Julianna and India sat under the big white tent on wooden chairs sipping lemonade while waiting for the ever-so-fun traditional bridal shower games to begin. Julianna looked up to see two people walking her way. The older lady was dark chocolate and had very striking facial features. She was wearing a sky-blue flowing maxi dress and she had long black hair that was pulled back in a ponytail. The younger lady was tall and thin but quite shapely. She was milk chocolate in color and had long black hair. Hers, however, had a center part and hung well past her shoulders. She was wearing a darker blue sundress with coordinating stiletto heels. As they got closer, Julianna recognized the younger lady. It was Gabi, a friend of hers from high school. Gabi graduated two years before Julianna, and they hadn't seen each other in three years. They were super excited to see each other.

"What are you doing here?" they said at the same time.

"This is my sister's bridal shower," said Julianna.

Gabi said, "This is my brother's fiancée's shower."

They both screamed, "OMG, we are going to be sisters!"

Gabi was Gabriella Daniels, Michael's younger sister and the lady she was with was their mother. How did that never come up before? Julianna had no idea, but it was great news!

Chapter 9
Drafted But Not

Ever since Julianna had known Dean, his focus had been on football. He was a wide receiver and ran track to make himself, faster for football. He ran every day and would run until he vomited and just couldn't go any further. Dean watched professional football, college football, and studied tapes of himself playing over and over again. He got lots of other exercise too because he, like many other football players, thought he could play every sport there was even though his football coach would have killed him if he ever found out.

Julianna wanted Dean to have a successful football career. However, every year that Dean played college football, Julianna secretly hoped that they would lose a few games. If they had a winning season, they would play in a bowl game. That would mean that instead of Dean being home for a few weeks over Christmas break, he would only be home for a few days.

During Dean's junior year in college, he was drafted by the Atlanta Falcons—tenth round, April 30. For Dean, this meant his lifelong dream was coming true. For Julianna, this meant that he would be less available than ever and definitely not for her senior prom. It sucked for her, but she was happy for him. Dean packed up his apartment at school and headed to Atlanta.

Each player received a group of tickets for each game. When the team was in a player's hometown, all the other players would give that player their tickets. The Atlanta Falcons' last regular season game was against the Detroit Lions, and Dean had a lot of tickets. He invited his family and friends and had two tickets reserved for Julianna. Julianna and Carmen went to the game. The seats were on the 50-yard line at the Pontiac Silverdome, so they could see everything. The game was going great; Atlanta was up 14 to 0. Then disaster struck in the third quarter. Dean took a helmet to his right knee, and he went down. Julianna gasped, and it felt like her heart stopped.

Julianna and the rest of Dean's guests were standing up waiting to see how he was doing. After a few minutes passed, Dean was back on his feet and limping off the field. The crowd clapped and took their seats. The doctor examined and iced Dean's knee. Julianna was sure that if they had been playing at any other venue, Dean would have been done for the night, but by the beginning of the fourth quarter, there he was running back on the field. With five minutes left until the end of the game, Dean took another blow to his knee. He didn't return to the field after that one. The final score of the game was Atlanta Falcons 20-6 over the Detroit Lions.

Dean and Julianna planned to go out after the game. Dean told Julianna to bring one of her friends and that he would do the same. Carmen and Julianna waited for Dean outside of the team locker room. One of the players exited the locker room and walked by them. This guy was so fine that Carmen, who was engaged, slipped her engagement ring off her finger and into her purse, just in case he was the guy that was joining them.

Dean emerged from the locker room and hugged and kissed Julianna. Dean said hey to Carmen, hugged her and introduced them both to Mr. Fine AKA Scott. Dean, Julianna, Carmen, and Scott made their way to the parking lot and to Julianna's car. They went down to Nikki's in Greektown. Dean had ice packs taped to his knee, but they all still had a good time.

Afterward, Julianna drove back to her house to drop Carmen off at her car. Julianna was going back to the team hotel with Dean. The team always put the guys two to a room, but Dean had arranged to switch rooms with the odd man out who got a room to himself.

When they got to the house, both Carmen and Scott got out of the car. At first Julianna thought that Scott was just being a gentleman and walking Carmen to her car, but then she saw Scott get into Carmen's car.

Julianna and Dean looked at each other and he said, "Well, it looks like Carmen is going with us."

They drove to the Holiday Inn off I-696 and I-75. Dean had to get a new room from the front desk because Scott had reclaimed his.

Both couples got into the elevator together. Dean and Julianna got off on the third floor. Before the doors closed, Julianna looked back at Carmen and asked, "¿Está bien?" (*Are you good?*)

"Sí, chica, estoy mejor que bien. Hasta mañana." (*Yes girl, I'm better than good. See you tomorrow.*)

"Buenas noches." (*Good night.*)

The elevator doors closed, and Julianna didn't see Carmen again until the next morning when Dean and Scott had to leave to catch the team bus to the airport.

Dean needed surgery on his knee. The following week, Julianna went to Georgia to be with him through the surgery and his recovery. It turned out that Dean would never play football again. The doctor said if Dean ever received that type of hit to his knee again, he would never walk properly.

Dean recovered from his knee surgery, and after four months of physical therapy, he was released from the team. He packed up and moved back to Indiana to finish his final year at Notre Dame. He called Julianna when he was ready to go and said that he would call her when he arrived in Indiana. Julianna told him to have a safe trip.

It was three months later when he finally called. He called like they had just spoken the day before.

"Happy Birthday! How's the love of my life?"

"Who is this?"

"This is Dean, stop playing!"

Julianna was hurt and pissed and wasn't trying to hear anything he had to say. She did catch that he said that he was back at school before she told him that she couldn't talk and had to go.

Dean didn't do a good job of balancing his grief from being cut and their relationship, and she didn't do a good job of being understanding. She knew that Dean was having a hard time dealing with no longer being able to play ball, but she just couldn't get over the fact that he shut her out for so long. They talked less and less over the next three months. By the time Julianna's sister Lisa got married, Julianna and Dean weren't talking at all. The silence between them felt heavier than the arguments ever had. That was the day that Julianna started seeing Anthony.

Chapter 10
Anthony Franklin

In the months that followed Lisa and Michael's wedding, Julianna spent all of her free time with Anthony. Julianna loved talking to Anthony. They spent hours talking about any and everything. When they weren't together, they talked on the telephone as much as possible. Julianna had never loved anyone's intellect before. His photographic memory and passion for history made him irresistible.

They had Thanksgiving dinner with Julianna's family and dessert with Anthony's family. Afterward, they went to Anthony's apartment and Julianna got to see all those muscles up close and personal. His chest was broad. His arms were huge; his legs were well

defined and rock hard. Anthony was Julianna's first—
and to her, he was worth the wait.

Saturday was Julianna's favorite day of the week
because it was their day. No matter how much time they
did or didn't spend together the rest of the week, they
knew that Saturday was just for them. They didn't care
what they did as long as they were together. Anthony
had to begin each day with a workout and a trip to get
some hot coffee, which Julianna referred to as his liquid
crack. Sometimes they would spend the day at
Julianna's house. They would make a meal together and
spend the day watching movies, often accompanied by
India, Jonathan, or her parents. Sometimes they hung
out with Lisa and Michael or Carmen and her fiancé.
One Saturday, Lisa and Michael showed up and
announced to the family that they were expecting a
baby. Lisa was due the following August.

India needed a licensed driver in the car to practice
her driving, and she was always able to get Anthony to
talk Julianna into taking her. They all went, but it was

risky to say the least. India turned the steering wheel when she was changing lanes like she was turning a corner. There was something about the training received by the students who attended Cass and took driver's training at Mumford that just wasn't right. Anthony was patient with India... Julianna, not so much, but she loved that about Anthony.

They spent time with Anthony's family as well. Julianna and Anthony's mother got along really well. She thought Julianna and Anthony were so much alike that she called them twins. They laughed at the same things and finished each other's sentences. They would even think to call his mother at the same time. Whenever Julianna called his mother, Anthony would have either just called or would call while they were still on the phone.

Some Saturdays were spent at Anthony's apartment. They read books together and discussed them or just listened to music. Their favorite place to eat was a Mediterranean restaurant named La Shish. They always had lentil soup along with the marinated charbroiled deboned chicken with almond rice and garlic sauce. They would sit in the restaurant eating and talking for hours.

Everything Anthony did made Julianna feel special—particularly the single red rose he gave her every time he saw her, and the thirteen red roses he gave her on August 8, their anniversary.

When she asked, "Why thirteen roses?"

He said, "Red roses, of course, because they are your favorite. One dozen roses because it's our anniversary, and I wanted to add an extra one to symbolize the year that we've been together."

Christmas of the following year, Anthony presented Julianna with a little red box. In the little box was a promise ring. It was a yellow gold band that dipped a little in the middle, like the bottom of a heart, and it had nine small round diamonds in it. He told her that he had enlisted in the Marine Corps.

He said, "I'm not expecting you not to date, but if you can be patient with me, I promise that I will be back for you. I need to do this; I need to go to the Corps so that I can be the man that I need to be. I only have love for you, and I have known since the night that we danced at Michael and Lisa's wedding that I would make you my wife one day, and I will."

Before he left town, Anthony stopped by Lisa and Michael's house to see Michael. Michael wasn't home, but unfortunately for Anthony, Lisa was. Lisa invited Anthony in and told him to take a seat.

She said, "I know that you gave Julianna that promise ring. I don't have a problem with you wanting to marry her when she gets older, but I know that you have not been completely honest with her—and that I do have a problem with. I understand that you may not feel that your little secret is relevant, but I need you to understand that there is no way that I'm going to allow you to marry my sister without her knowing. If you ever actually propose to her, you'd better tell her, or I will!"

Anthony had to figure out a way to tell Julianna. He had wanted to be with her for so long.

Chapter 11
Anthony's Jewel

Anthony…

One day, a few years before Michael and Lisa got married, I was with Michael when he went by Lisa's house. I met Lisa's sisters, Julianna and India, and her brother Jonathan. We all hung out for a couple of hours and watched the movie *Beverly Hills Cop*. Michael was bragging because Eddie Murphy wore a Mumford Phys. Ed. Dept. t-shirt in the movie. Lisa and India stayed out of it because apparently Michael and Julianna had some kind of ongoing Cooley-Mumford rivalry going on between them. I thought that Julianna was beautiful back then. When we left, I asked Mike to hook me up with her. I damn near choked when he told me that she was only 16 years old. I quickly left that subject alone.

When Julianna walked into the room at the wedding, let's just say that I needed a few minutes before I could stand up. I watched her direct the wedding, and I just couldn't take my eyes off her all day. I know this might sound a little extreme, but when she caught the bouquet and then I caught the garter, I thought that it was a sign that we were supposed to be together. When she was finished working, I couldn't wait to ask her to dance. Once I held her in my arms, I knew that she was the one for me. What I feel for her is beyond anything I can put into words.

I hated to leave her, but I needed to handle my business as a man. I wanted her to wait for me, but I knew that it was too much to ask. I had to trust that if we belonged together, the way that I believed we did, it would all work itself out.

Chapter 12
The Forces of Nature

Julianna heard the chimes of the doorbell, and then she heard Jonathan call out to her, "Jewels, company!"

Julianna went down the stairs, and there he was standing proud and looking good. He was wearing a midnight blue uniform coat with red trim; there were ribbons on the left and gold buttons that had little eagles and anchors on them. The coat had a high collar and a white belt with a gold buckle with an eagle, a globe, and an anchor. His arm held a patch with his Lance Corporal rank; he was wearing white gloves and held a crisp white hat. There was a solid red stripe running down the outside of each leg of his sky-blue trousers that rested perfectly on top of his shiny black dress shoes.

Julianna hugged him and said, "Oh my God, Anthony, it's so good to see you. What are you... when did you get home?"

"I've been here less than twenty-four hours. Please excuse the lack of notice, but I wanted to surprise you. Go get dressed, I'm taking you out."

"How did you even know I would be here?"

"I had it on good authority that you would be available." Then he looked over, smiled, and nodded at the already smiling Ms. Busybody India, who ran down the stairs behind Julianna.

"I'm just about ready anyway, because I thought that India and I were going out to dinner with Michael and Lisa. Now I can see that it was all a part of this secret mission you had her on, so give me fifteen minutes."

Julianna smiled and shook her head as she went up the stairs, glancing back to sneak a peek at Anthony just in time to see the high five between him and India.

She returned in a red tea length halter dress with matching strappy three-inch heel sandals. He took her to *The Whitney*. It was a Romanesque style mansion turned restaurant located on Woodward Avenue. It was one of, if not the finest, restaurants in Detroit. They went through the front doors to a breathtaking space called the Great Hall. It had a beautiful wooden ceiling with multiple crystal chandeliers, a grand piano, and a huge fireplace. They could see the entrance to six different rooms.

The hostess greeted them, "Good evening, Lance Corporal Franklin, Ms. Jeffries."

Anthony said, "Good evening" and touched Julianna on her lower back to signal that she should follow the hostess. Julianna smiled and wondered how the hostess knew their names. They were escorted up the grand staircase to the third floor to the Ghost Bar. It is called that because the mansion was rumored to be haunted. Two champagne glasses were delivered to them. Julianna felt the bubbles on her tongue, and then realized that they were drinking Moët.

About twenty minutes later, the hostess returned and asked them to follow her. They went back down the stairs to the first floor. They entered a room called the Reception Room. It was dark cream with white trim and pink chairs; it had a fabulous white fireplace topped with a Venetian style mirror. The room was filled with candles and only had one table in it. In the center of the table was a bouquet of fourteen red roses. Anthony held Julianna's seat for her and then moved his chair next to her. He sat down and they were served a delicious five course meal. They talked and laughed and had a great time.

They both had blue crab and roasted red pepper bisque; flash fried calamari; classic Caesar salads; twin lobster tails with herbed rice and grilled asparagus with drawn butter.

Just after the delivery of the fifth course, which was white chocolate strawberry tortes, Anthony got really serious.

"Baby... talking on the phone, writing letters, even the visits are just not enough anymore. I can't wait any longer."

"For what?"

"For you to be my wife." Anthony pulled out a little blue box. Julianna read the words *Tiffany & Co.* He opened the blue box and pulled out a black velvet box, then he dropped down to one knee. The black box held a two-carat marquise solitaire diamond engagement ring... "Two years ago today, I saw you at Michael and Lisa's wedding, and I knew that you would be my wife. I love you with all my heart. I think that we are perfect for each other. Will you marry me?"

Julianna could barely hear what Anthony was saying over the sound of her heartbeat. She could feel the excitement building inside of her as she said, "Yes!"

Chapter 13
The Secret

Julianna was excited to share the news of her engagement with everyone. Her family loved Anthony, so the announcement went well. Mostly anyway… Lisa seemed to be acting a little funny, but she said all the right things, so Julianna overlooked it. Besides, Lisa was always being overprotective. Not to mention the fact that it was August, Lisa was nine months pregnant, and she hated the heat on a normal day. India was happy but wasn't surprised at all… clearly, she knew what was going to happen. There were lots of congratulations, oohs and aahs over the ring, and hugs; Julianna even saw Lisa hug Anthony.

What she missed was what Lisa whispered in Anthony's ear, "Don't forget what I told you... you tell her, or I will!"

Julianna couldn't wait to put the whole wedding together. Anthony had to go back to California, so the planning would mostly be up to her. He was stationed at Camp Pendleton in San Diego, and they were going to live off-base there until he could get approved for on-base housing.

Julianna had been working at the *University of Michigan Hospital* planning fundraising events, but she and her sisters also had their own company. Julianna, Lisa, and India created a wedding planning company, and named it *Affairs of the Heart*. After the success of Lisa's wedding, Julianna realized that her passion was in planning and directing weddings. The skills that Lisa learned working in the flower shop allowed her to design and create flowers for the weddings. India's knack for interfering and need to be in the center of all the action made her the perfect person to handle the people who were a part of the wedding parties and make sure everyone was ready, in place, and on time.

Julianna knew that she and her sisters could create the perfect wedding. The wedding wouldn't be too big, and of course, Lisa and Michael would be the matron of honor and best man. India, Carmen, Gabi, William, and Autumn would also be part of the wedding party. Anthony was the only boy, but he had four sisters. Julianna got along really well with his sister Kristina, so she thought it would be nice to include her.

The wedding planning continued. Julianna and Carmen picked out dresses and looked at venues all over the Detroit Metropolitan area. While Carmen was also engaged and had been for a while, she and her fiancé had yet to set a date. So, no one thought that it was actually going to happen.

Julianna wanted to make sure that she included Anthony's family in the planning as much as possible. His mom was a jazz singer, so Julianna asked her if she would sing during the ceremony. His dad had passed away some years ago, and Julianna wanted to do something special to acknowledge him. Julianna began to visit Anthony's mom frequently. The house was usually full of family…his mom, his sisters, nieces, and nephews.

Julianna was visiting with Kristina at his mom's house. Julianna was showing off pictures of Lisa's baby, Mikey, when out of the blue Anthony's niece Latrice said, "Hopefully Ashley will be able to come to the wedding."

Kristina yelled, "LATRICE!"

Julianna said, "Who?"

Latrice said, "Ashley, Uncle Anthony's daughter."

Julianna had a momentary brain freeze, but she didn't want Latrice to know that she had never even heard of this daughter of his, so she said, "Yeah, hopefully."

Kristina just watched and waited, and since Julianna didn't say anything about it, neither did she. Within the next thirty minutes, Julianna excused herself and left the house.

Julianna couldn't get to a telephone quick enough. She was able to reach Anthony, which almost never happened right away.

"Who is Ashley?"

Anthony was quiet for a minute and said, "Lisa told you?"

"Lisa knows?"

"Okay Julianna, this is what happened. When I was 16, I had sex for the first time. It was her first time too, and she got pregnant. I didn't particularly want her to keep the baby, but there wasn't anything I could do about it. After she had the baby, she thought that we should get married. We were only 17, and I wasn't going to get married just because she had a baby. She told me that if I didn't marry her that I would never see the baby again. I didn't marry her, and I haven't seen the baby in seven years."

"So why didn't you just tell me?"

"Because at first it was too soon, then all of a sudden it was too late. I didn't know how to tell you."

"So, you thought it would be better that I hear it from Latrice?"

"Latrice told you?"

"Yeah, but it doesn't even matter. What matters is that it wasn't you who told me. Forget the fact that we've been together for two years. Before you planned the proposal, you should have planned on telling me about your daughter. Certainly, in the three months that we've been engaged, you could have found a way to bring it up. If you can keep something like this from me, clearly, we are not in a place where we need to be talking about getting married. Goodbye Anthony!" Julianna hung up the phone. She heard the phone ringing as she was leaving the house. She kept going.

Julianna sat in her car staring at her engagement ring.

The car was silent.

The engine wasn't even on.

The ring caught the late afternoon light.

For a split second, she wondered if loving him was worth forgiving him—and she hated herself for even thinking it.

Julianna arrived at Lisa's house. Lisa answered the door and saw the look on Julianna's face.

"Come in, what's wrong?"

"You knew this whole time?"

"Knew what?"

"Ashley!"

"Jewels, look, when you first started seeing each other I didn't know if it was serious. But I told him back then that if you two got serious, that he had to tell you, or I would. When he proposed, I told him again. I felt like he should be the one to tell you, but you have to know that I would never have let you walk into a marriage blind. What are you going to do?"

"I already talked to Anthony, but I'm not trying to hear his excuses, he should have told me. The wedding is off! I can't believe that he put his own fear of my reaction ahead of my feelings. He didn't bother to take the time to consider how his actions would affect me."

"You might want to slow down before you make any big decisions. It might be too soon for you to be objective about this. I'm not taking his side or saying that he wasn't wrong, I just know how much you love him. Before you give everything up you might want to consider the possibility that you are overreacting to this."

"What!? Overreacting! How is it that I'm overreacting, he's the one who can't be trusted?"

"I know that you don't like to talk about it, but you have your own secret, that unless something has changed, he doesn't know about."

"Lisa! That doesn't have anything to do with him."

"But it does, Jewels. It's playing into how you're dealing with this situation and all your trust issues in general. I'm just saying that while it is not the same thing as this, it's definitely something that your future husband should know about you. Since you feel so justified in keeping your secret, maybe you can see why he did the same thing."

"It's different Lisa! I don't even want to think about Anthony right now. Dean has been calling me; I should just go ahead and talk to him."

Chapter 14
Yes, But No, But Yes, But No

It had been a year since the whole Anthony engagement debacle, and Julianna had been seeing and talking to Dean regularly. Julianna realized that she had a habit of being rather unforgiving. Julianna would talk to Anthony, but she was not in a place of moving past what happened. Not even after all the conversations, explanations, or the arrival of the regularly scheduled rose delivery that was now up to fifteen roses.

Julianna was ready to consider the fact that maybe, just maybe she overreacted with Dean. Julianna and Dean continued to reconnect, but the same issue kept coming up. Dean was definitely not interested in moving back to Detroit. Their relationship had moved to the next level, and he wanted Julianna to move to

Indiana to be with him. Since they started talking again, Julianna and Dean saw each other almost every weekend. One weekend she would drive to Indiana, the next weekend he would drive to Detroit, but the distance was taking its toll on both of them. Julianna felt as though they had dealt with the long-distance relationship long enough. She decided it was time to move to Indiana with Dean. While Julianna's family was fond of Dean, they were not in favor of their idea to shack up. That definitely lost him some fans in the family. Lisa was a borderline fan at best, but India was all the way with Team Anthony, so she had no love for Dean. And he was taking her big sister away from her too! Forget about it… Dean's chances of ever winning over India were slim to none.

Dean flew home to get Julianna. When Julianna opened the door to let Dean in, he was standing on the porch with a big smile on his face. Julianna noticed that his braces were gone, and his teeth were perfectly straight. Although Julianna didn't think it was possible, Dean was even better looking than he was before.

Dean had picked up a U-Haul truck before he got to Julianna's house. William, Jonathan, and a reluctant Michael helped him pack up the truck with all of Julianna's belongings.

Michael didn't think that Dean was a bad guy, but he had two issues with the situation. He believed that if Dean was serious about being with Julianna, that he would have married her. The second issue was that he felt like Julianna hadn't dealt with her feelings for Anthony and they still had unfinished business. He privately told Lisa that this situation was not going to end well.

Julianna said her goodbyes to her family, and she and Dean left Detroit and drove the three and a half hours to South Bend, Indiana. Dean had some of his friends waiting to help unload the truck. His lease on his apartment was up a month before and on her last visit, they signed a lease on a townhouse. Dean had been in

Indiana for quite some time, so he had everything he needed but he did live like a bachelor. Julianna wanted all the comforts of home... everything, down to the spoon rest for the stove. After everything was unloaded and everyone was gone, Julianna went to the freezer and pulled out a bottle of champagne that she put there when they first arrived. They decided to save the unpacking for the morning; they would spend the night celebrating their first night together.

With the exception of the days when Julianna couldn't figure out why Dean seemed to be purposely starting arguments with her, things were really good between them. Dean had been coaching at the University of Notre Dame since he graduated. Julianna was a wedding planner at the Marriott Hotel in South Bend, and she also still had events to manage in Michigan, so she went back about once a month.

Every time she went home, Julianna would find a letter waiting at her parents' house from Anthony. She would write him back or call while she was in Detroit. They also would meet at La Shish for dinner on the rare occasions that they were in town at the same time.

Dean was a huge college football fan, and he loved New Orleans. His team wasn't playing so the weekend after Thanksgiving, they went to New Orleans for the Bayou Classic. They went to the step show on Friday night, and on Saturday they went to the annual football game between Grambling State University and Southern University. It was a great day. There was a crowd of over 70,000 people at the Louisiana Superdome, and this was the first year the game was televised. Dean was happy about the score; Grambling won 25 to 13. Julianna enjoyed the game, but she was much more interested in the Battle of Bands at half time.

They had a wonderful Christmas. Dean surprised Julianna with a gold Gucci watch that she had her eye on for quite a while and airline tickets to New Orleans for Mardi Gras in February. That trip was almost like going to a totally different location from Bayou Classic.

During the day they walked the Riverwalk, went to the museums, and shops on Bourbon Street, and rode the streetcar uptown to the daiquiri shop. The daiquiri shop was like going into *31 Flavors*; there were a ridiculous amount of frozen daiquiri combinations available. At night they enjoyed the restaurants, the Mardi Gras parades, the famous Hurricane drinks, and the whole French Quarter experience, not to mention the Prince Conti Hotel where they were staying.

Dean had gotten verbally abusive, and it was progressively getting worse and was occurring more frequently. When he yelled, there was something different in his eyes—something she didn't recognize.

A month after their return from New Orleans, Julianna and Dean were having one of many arguments that Dean started for no apparent reason when Dean grabbed Julianna's breast.

It wasn't playful. It wasn't teasing. It was ownership. And for a split second, she told herself that maybe this was just how intense love felt.

"STOP!"

"You belong to me, and I can have you whenever I want." Dean grabbed her again.

Julianna took the Mardi Gras beads that were lying on the bed and swung them at him, hitting him across his face. Dean walked over to her and punched her in her thigh.

As Dean walked out of the room, Julianna said, "You hit like a BITCH!"

Julianna never liked to let him know when he hurt her. She cried as she laid the heating pad on her leg. She knew that she was making it worse by fighting back, but she couldn't figure out what she was doing that was making him so angry in the first place. Julianna thought that it would please Dean if he knew that he actually hurt her, so she hid the bruise from him for the weeks that it took to go away.

As always, after things got out of hand, Dean was being really sweet to Julianna. Julianna wasn't feeling well; she was tired and running to the bathroom all the time and she was nauseous, so she decided to go to the doctor.

When Dean got home from work, Julianna said, "Hey Dean, do you remember our trip to New Orleans?"

"Of course, why?"

"Well do you remember the night we went to dinner at *Delachaise*; all the drinks and all the ... dessert?"

"I remember that night, it was great!"

"Okay, well you know how I haven't been feeling well?"

"Yeah, Babe, but what does that have to do with— Oh, shit! ... What are you saying?"

"I'm saying that we're having a baby."

The words hung in the air.

She had always believed love was something you chose. This felt like something choosing her.

Dean was quiet for a few minutes. Then he hugged her, and then repeatedly expressed his desire to have a son.

During Julianna's pregnancy, she and Dean got into another verbal altercation that escalated when they both lost their tempers. Dean was yelling at her, and when Julianna kept arguing back at him, he walked past where she was sitting and hit her in her throat. Julianna gasped, but she was too stubborn to admit when she was hurt so she just sucked it up and didn't say anything. Later that evening, Dean was on the couch watching television. Julianna was tired of him putting his hands on her. She saw her chance, so she went over to the couch and with all of her weight, she dropped her elbow into his throat. Dean jumped up, grabbed Julianna around her neck, and they both went over the back of the couch heads first. Julianna got away from him and ran to the back of the house. He caught her and wrapped his hands back around her throat and choked her. Even though she was getting lightheaded, she wouldn't stop talking.

"So, what are you going to do now, kill me? Do it! I wish you would. Then you know what? My father will be down here looking for you. Yeah, I know you don't want that. So, what are you going to do?"

He just looked at her, pushed her into the wall again and walked away.

"Yeah, that's what I thought!"

Julianna went into the bathroom, locked the door and turned on the water. She put the top down on the toilet seat, sat down and cried. It had never been that bad before, and Julianna was starting to fear what would happen next.

Julianna told Dean that she was not going to fight and be stressed out all the time while she was pregnant; she was concerned about the effect it would have on the baby. She told him that if he put his hands on her again, that she would leave and go back home. He agreed to control his anger.

Dean always left Julianna to handle all the business of running the household. They weren't getting along. So, when it was time to renew the lease, her pen hovered over the blank line.

That's when she did it—put it in her name only.

He trusted her to handle the paperwork. He never thought to ask whose name was on it. It wasn't about kicking him out. It was about knowing she could—if she ever had to.

During a weekly phone call between Lisa, Julianna, and India, India said, "Jewels, Anthony sent you roses today… sixteen of them!"

"Wow, yeah, I have to tell Anthony about the baby. I can't do it in a letter and especially not while he's still in Saudi Arabia. I'm going to have to wait for him to come home."

Lisa said, "What's the problem? It's not like you two are together or something."

"I know, but you know we're still close, and he's still on this mission that ends with the two of us being together. So, I'm just not sure how he's going to take it. I don't want to hurt him, Lisa!"

India chimed in, "Yeah Lisa, she doesn't want to hurt him!"

Lisa chuckled and said, "Okay, whatever!"

Julianna went to all her scheduled prenatal visits to her doctor. Three months later during a routine visit, she explained that her energy was pretty low. The doctor hooked her up to the fetal monitor and explained that the reason she was feeling that way was because she was in labor. The doctor admitted her and after nothing happened over the course of eight hours, the doctor sent her home. She told her to come back at 9:00 AM because the baby was definitely coming the next day. At 5:00 AM the following morning, Julianna woke Dean up because she thought she was having contractions. They laid in bed and talked while she continued to have contractions every five minutes. After thirty minutes she decided that they should get to the hospital. At 1:14 PM Julianna gave birth to David Lawson.

Julianna's mother arrived the same day that she had David and stayed for the first ten days to help with the baby. Three days after her mother left, Lisa arrived. She left her son at home with Michael, and she told Julianna that she was pretty sure that she was pregnant again. Lisa stayed for ten days as well. On the third day of Lisa's visit, Julianna started getting sick. She was having bad cramps and could barely hold David. She figured out that she could control the pain by adjusting her diet. As long as she ate chicken noodle soup and crackers and drank ginger ale, the pain went away.

Over the next twelve days after Lisa left, Julianna continued to experience pain. One day Julianna woke up in so much pain that Dean asked if he should stay home from work. Julianna told him that she would be fine and that he should go ahead to work. Within the next three hours, Julianna's pain was worse than ever. She took a cab to the hospital. The nurses took care of David until Dean could get there. The ultrasound showed that Julianna's gallbladder was inflamed. The doctor told her that they needed to operate right away. Julianna was concerned about Dean's ability to take care of David. She asked if she could go back to Michigan to have the surgery. The doctor explained that there wasn't time for her to drive home and that if she got on an airplane the altitude would cause her gallbladder to burst. She needed emergency surgery; it was also too late for her to have laser surgery; she would have a three-inch scar from the traditional surgery.

Julianna had her surgery and was in the hospital for six days. Dean called her parents to let them know what was going on. They told him that they would send India to help. Dean was able to take care of David until India arrived. Julianna was released from the hospital on Christmas Eve. When she left, she had internal stitches, external staples and a tube hanging out of her stomach. India helped Julianna around the house and took care of David; she was able to stay until after the New Year when she had to get back for school. Julianna and India went for walks daily with David. He was such a beautiful baby that people thought he was a girl. One day they were in the mall, and they were sitting on a bench so Julianna could rest. This lady sat next to them and couldn't stop raving about how beautiful David was. Then she got up and went into a toy store. When the lady returned, she gave Julianna a stuffed animal for David. She said that she just couldn't help herself.

Dean was sick with a cold, but he wouldn't take any medicine. He believed that vitamin C was the cure for everything. He was upstairs resting, and he had the heat turned up to 80 degrees. Julianna was downstairs with David watching television under the ceiling fan. Dean decided that he wanted to go downstairs and watch television. He wanted to keep the heat turned up, and he wanted Julianna to turn the ceiling fan off. Julianna understood that he was cranky, and she wanted Dean to be comfortable, but it was more important to her that the baby be at a comfortable temperature. They took turns turning the fan on and off until Dean stood up and actually held the blades of the fan so that they could no longer spin. They stood under the fan arguing. During the argument, Dean tried to snatch David from Julianna. When Julianna pulled away, Dean got irate.

"Don't ever try to keep my son from me!"

"I'm not keeping him from you, but I'm not going to give him to you when you are out of control." Julianna turned to walk away.

When her back was to Dean, he pushed her. She flew past the glass coffee table. Fortunately, she was able to hold on to David, or he would have fallen through the glass. She was falling forward, so in order not to fall on David she had to spin around. As she twisted, she could feel the stitches rip but she was able to avoid falling on David.

When she hit the couch, she was DONE: DONE with the fighting; DONE with the lying; DONE with the cheating; DONE with the abuse; she was DONE with Dean. She sat on the couch, and he sat on the stairs across from her.

"When I leave, you don't have to worry, I will never keep you or your family away from David."

"Leave if you want to leave; don't let it be said that I held you up."

"Oh, I will." In that moment it all became clear to her. She would wait until she got her income tax refund, and she and David would head back to Michigan.

Everything was quite civil after that. There was no more arguing, they just went through their day-to-day life in the same house; just not together. Julianna's dad came to town on business and was able to meet his grandson David for the first time. Julianna cooked a big meal filled with all her dad's favorite things. Before he left, he gave Julianna an envelope with an airline ticket in it. It was a round-trip ticket back to Detroit. He said that he wanted her to be able to go back for a visit. Julianna hadn't told her family that she was leaving Dean yet, so her father had no idea what good timing this was. Julianna made some calls and had a meeting lined up. A few weeks later, Julianna and David went to Detroit.

Lisa and India picked them up at the airport and hung out with them most of the time. Julianna visited with her family, and she also made a point to visit with Dean's family because they hadn't seen David. Julianna usually got along well with Dean's mother, but his mother was not happy that when Julianna left, she took David with her. Dean's mom was a first-time grandmother and understandably wanted to spend time with her grandson, but she wanted to keep him the whole time Julianna was in town. Julianna tried to explain that this was their first visit home, and she couldn't go anywhere without David because almost no one had seen him, but his mom was not trying to hear it.

Julianna's meeting went well, and she was going to be returning to her job at the hospital. It also worked out that she would be returning to the house on Abington. Julianna and Carmen met Autumn and William for dinner at the Red Lobster on Plymouth off Middlebelt Road. She told them how Dean had been calling since she got to Detroit. He wanted to let her know that he missed them and that he wanted to try and work things out. "He sounded sincere, but they always are after it's too late."

Julianna and David returned to Indiana. Dean was being as sweet as pie. His emotions about the move had run a full spectrum—acting like he didn't care, then being angry, then begging her to stay. Today was a begging day. Once Julianna explained that she wasn't interested in working it out, he stopped fighting it. When Julianna's tax refund arrived, she was ready to go. She had everything lined up, the job, the house, and the moving team. She made the call and a week later India,

Carmen, Autumn, and William showed up. The townhouse was in her name, so when she left, Dean had to go, too. Julianna left him with what he had when she got there and a few additional things. They packed up her things, closed the townhouse, and turned in the keys. That night, they all stayed at Dean's new apartment.

The next morning, they said goodbye to Dean and left for Detroit. William drove the truck back, and the ladies and David rode back in Carmen's car. Julianna looked out of the back window as they pulled away. Dean was bent over the balcony rail, watching what should have been his family drive away.

Part Four:

Lunacy

Chapter 15
Kay Elle Goode

Julianna...

The Monday following my return to Detroit, I started back to work at the University of Michigan. For the most part, it was a smooth transition back. There was a young lady who was now working in my department who wasn't there before. Kay Elle Goode was 4'9", petite, chocolate, pretty and she presented as super sweet. She had a high-pitched voice, and she always wore soft pink. Kay Elle's work was directly related to Education, and she didn't feel like there was any need for the directive that was given that everything go through my office.

Not to mention the fact that Kay Elle's opinion was that I was only hired because I was friends with our Director. As Kay Elle wasn't a fan of the Director, that was reason enough not to like me. None of that sweetness that Kay Elle exuded was aimed at me; she wasn't feeling me at all. And if you called her Kay, she would quickly let you know that she preferred Kay Elle. She wasn't the first woman to dislike me without cause. So as soon as I caught the shade that Kay Elle was throwing my way, I adapted and was over Kay Elle. All that super sweet, chipper (yes, chipper) conversation first thing in the morning was too much for me anyway. It was like having to deal with a hyped-up cheerleader every day.

Kay Elle...

There was a fundraising event at the University of Michigan for the Annual Fund. This was the biggest event of the year and because it was an evening function, significant others were invited. My fiancé Tim and I made our way to the event. When we arrived, I saw some friends that I knew, and Tim had met most of my co-workers before, so we were all greeting each other. With my back to Tim, I heard a shout of familiarity:

"Julianna Jeffries – is that you?" Tim called out.

"Heyyyyyyyyyyyyyyyyy Tim Richards!" she said, just as excited. As I turned to look, they were heading for an embrace which lasted longer than I preferred. To be absolutely honest, any time was longer than I preferred. Tim asked what Julianna was doing there and she told him that she worked for the hospital.

"What are you doing here?" Julianna asked Tim.

"My fiancée works here."

"Oh really, who is your fiancée?"

As Tim opened his mouth to say my name, I posted my fake smile on my face, and I walked up to them and asked how they knew each other. Tim began to explain that they went to high school together, in the most excited tone I'd ever heard come out of his mouth. I held back my "oh great, another Cooley Cardinal" and continued to listen. He went on and on and on talking about Julianna Jeffries and how they were so cool in high school. They went on to exchange "remember when" stories as I stood there in disbelief that he seemed to simply adore the one person whom I liked the least.

Eventually the program started, and my ears could be relieved of them reliving their high school days. After the event, I said my goodbyes and made a mad dash for the door. I, however, had to go back and pull Tim away from Julianna. When we got in the car, not only did Tim talk nonstop about just how cool Julianna is and how much he loves her – but he actually stopped by his mom's house to get his high school yearbook to show me all of the pictures of Julianna. At this point, I had to ask if they had a thing for each other or ever dated. He said no, but not emphatically enough for me, so I continued to press him and ask if they ever had a relationship. He finally convinced me that they never ever had anything going on, but what happened next made me doubt him again. As soon as we reached my house, he told me to come over and he proceeded to tell me every detail about every event for every picture she was in. And she was on several pages in the yearbook. Several. Way more than I ever wanted to see. And how exactly did he know what pages of the yearbook she was on? I'm just saying that it was suspect.

Julianna…

It turned out that Kay Elle and I actually got along quite well. Before we knew it, we were taking our breaks and lunches together; we even hung out after work. Kay Elle was nothing like I thought. Kay Elle grew up on Linwood and Davison and went to Central High School. This was no bougie private school girl from the suburbs—Kay Elle was straight out of the hood. She grew up thinking that she would never go to college. She heard her father tell her brothers that they couldn't afford college. She figured that she would get pregnant and be on welfare because that's what the girls in her neighborhood did.

She got good grades in school, so her counselor called Kay Elle into her office to discuss her future. Kay Elle explained about her father's philosophy on college. The counselor said that she understood but that Kay Elle should fill out an application for the Coleman A. Young Foundation Scholarship. Kay Elle received that scholarship and a few more. She ended up getting both a bachelor's degree and a master's degree from Marygrove College; a $71,000 education with only $3,000 out of pocket. Kay from Linwood and Davison transformed into Kay Elle and made her way to the University of Michigan to make sure that young people had all the money that they needed for college.

Chapter 16
Craig Goodwin

Julianna…

I had just moved back to Detroit from Indiana. I was hanging out at Autumn's mother's house and Autumn's brother Craig was there.

"Hey Julianna, when can I take you out?"

"Hold on, let me talk to Autumn for a minute." I went in the other room, and I said, "Autumn, what's up with that whole Michigan's Most Wanted thing?"

"Oh, I thought I told you about that. The police were watching him at the Residence Inn. Somehow, they were able to see into his room, so the one time he put his gun down, they entered the room and were waiting for him when he came out of the bathroom. They arrested him and he was in jail for a few months on murder charges but when all the witnesses in his case either disappeared or changed their story, the police had no choice but to drop the charges and release him."

While I wasn't exactly interested in dating Craig, we always got along well and it was time to eat. I was over the whole love thing anyway, and Autumn was pushing me to go so I figured why not. Craig and I went to dinner and had a really nice time; I had forgotten that Craig was such a cool person. We went to my favorite restaurant, Red Lobster. I loved the food, and we had a great conversation. Craig drove me home and walked me to my door. I thanked him for a good time. As he moved in for the good night kiss, I turned my head just enough for him to get my cheek instead of my lips.

Craig was 5'11" and he had a deep dark chocolate complexion. His skin was smooth and flawless, and he had big pretty hazel eyes. His jawline was strong which gave him a very masculine look. Craig paid attention to every detail of his appearance. His haircut was a low-cut Caesar with the deep waves that was always perfectly lined. And he was always dressed casually fine; his outfits always looked like they were brand new. He was into the science of women. He always knew exactly what a woman wanted to hear and whatever it was, he would tell her. Craig was the type of guy who had women chasing him. He didn't call women, they called him. He didn't request to see them, they begged to see him. I knew all about his rules, and while I liked him, it just really wasn't that serious to me, so I broke all of them (a phenomenon which he had probably never experienced because he came all off his game). He started calling me regularly asking me to go out with him. I did enjoy his company, so most of the time I said yes.

There were many perks to dating Craig. After visits with him, I would get home and find that he had put money in my pockets. Since Autumn encouraged me to go out with Craig, I usually gave her a cut of whatever money he gave me. Craig had many connections that provided him with the things he required. He could get anything from tags for license plates to a completely different identity. He also could get any type of clothing that he wanted. Whatever I wanted, Craig wanted for me. Craig would take me shopping and have me try on the clothes that I liked. I would leave them in the fitting room, as instructed, and by the time I got home, whatever I left would be hanging in my closet.

Craig was still married to Donna. They hadn't lived together as far back as I could remember, but clearly, they were still having sex because Donna was six months pregnant, with twins. I didn't want to marry him, and I wasn't having sex with him, so it didn't bother me. Donna could not stand the fact that I was dating Craig. Normally this would be how one would expect the wife to act, but I had witnessed Donna deal with, even cook for other women in Craig's life. So, I just didn't understand what Donna's problem was with me.

The backstory with them was that Craig loved Donna and proposed to her. Donna said yes, but only in the hopes that some other guy she really wanted to be with would get jealous and want her for himself — which never happened. Craig and Donna got married, had Craig Jr. (who everyone called CJ) and everything was fine until Craig found out about the other guy. He took her wedding rings from her, took CJ and moved out and on with his life. When she tried to confront the other women in his life and tell them that she was married to Craig, he denied it to her face. There was nothing she could do about it, so she just dealt with the other women.

I knew that Craig was into the drug life, but I didn't have anything to do with it. He never had it around me, and I never asked him anything about it. The only thing I saw was the money. The actual drugs weren't an issue because it wasn't like he was out in the streets selling them himself. He had people who had people who sold the drugs. I didn't know what Autumn's actual involvement was, but I'd seen her counting serious amounts of money on several occasions.

Autumn was a model and had some pretty serious gigs, up to and including New York Fashion Week, but lived well beyond anything she could have been making modeling. Whatever was going on, I didn't want to know. I didn't deal with Autumn and Craig together. When I was with Autumn, we did our friend thing. When I was with Craig, we did various things, none of which had anything to do with Autumn.

My telephone rang. It was Autumn. "I'm moving to New York and I'm leaving Friday."

"But it's Wednesday. What's going on?"

"You told me that you didn't want to know anything about this kind of stuff."

I knew that I said that I didn't want to know anything about what was going on with them, but if Autumn thought things were so bad that she needed to leave town, maybe it was time I listened.

"Okay, Autumn, I'm ready... just talk to me."

I sat quietly as Autumn told me the events of the past few months... Autumn convinced Ethan, her ex-boyfriend, and Craig to put their money together to pay for a shipment of drugs from California. Autumn's most recent boyfriend, who lived in California was supposed to deliver the package. The boyfriend came to Detroit, picked up the money, went back to California to get the product, but never returned to Detroit. Now Ethan's and Craig's money was gone. There was no product, and the boyfriend was missing. Craig was upset about the money, but there wasn't anything that he could do. He kind of just had to suck it up and take the loss. Ethan, on the other hand, wasn't as understanding.

Although he used to date Autumn and didn't have a problem with her, he and Craig had been enemies for many years. He decided that Craig and Autumn conspired to take his money. He told Autumn that if she didn't get him his money that he was going to kill her. Autumn went to Craig who came up with a plan. Craig told Autumn to invite Ethan over to her place, a high-rise apartment building in downtown Detroit. When Ethan got outside of Autumn's building, the hitman shot at him but missed. Ethan got away and then knew that Autumn set him up. At that point, he didn't care about the money, he was going to kill her. That's why she had to leave town.

The following month, Craig went to the old neighborhood to visit a friend who had been convicted of a crime and was scheduled to turn himself in to do his time in prison. Craig, who was on his motorcycle, his friend, and some other people were outside talking when an SUV with tinted windows came down the street. When the SUV got near them, it slowed down, the back driver's side window was lowered, and a man opened fire on them.

Autumn called me from New York to tell me that Craig had been shot. I went to Providence Hospital but wasn't allowed to see him... Donna was finally in a position to pull rank and she did. Craig was shot in the leg, and it was broken in several places. He had a cast on his left leg from his ankle to the top of his thigh. It was an attack by Ethan but not being in a position to run, Craig couldn't do anything about it until his leg healed. The question was how could he heal and get at Ethan before Ethan finished him off.

When Craig was released from the hospital he went to a hotel, but the conversation continued around where he could recuperate. The problem was that Ethan knew where everyone lived, everyone but me. I met Ethan when Autumn was dating him, but I knew he was in the life, so I didn't spend much time around him.

Craig's mother had the not so brilliant idea for Craig to stay at my house. I wasn't crazy about the idea, mostly because our relationship was nowhere near something of that magnitude. However, after lengthy discussions with him and his family, I was convinced that the best option for his safety was to stay with me. The one condition was that he stayed away from the old neighborhood, so that he couldn't be followed back to my house.

Craig gave me the bullets that the doctors removed from his leg. They were bronze in color and flat like they had been run over by a car. I presumed that it was supposed to be some kind of gangster bonding sentiment.

Having Craig at the house turned out not to be so bad. CJ was five and David was six months old. CJ was a really sweet child, he was really good with David. I loved it whenever he was around. Craig and I weren't playing house or anything; it was just nice when we were all together. In between Donna calling with her drama and various situations with whatever random chick Craig was using to get what he needed... everything between us was cool.

One day I said that I was going out but failed to mention that I was going to dinner with Anthony. It was the first time I had seen Anthony since I got pregnant and had David and I had to tell him. I knew that I hadn't cheated on Anthony, but I still felt guilty. As I told my story of Dean and David, Anthony looked me in my eyes and didn't say a word. His reaction was not what I expected. He wasn't upset about David at all. He was fuming about Dean putting his hands on me. Then I had to turn around and explain why Craig was at my house.

To that, Anthony simply said, "I'm just a phone call away. I love you, Julianna. If you ever need me for anything, call me and I promise I will be there."

Craig questioned me about coming in at 1:00 AM from dinner, but I didn't feel the need to explain, which Craig didn't like.

"You must still be seeing Dean, and if I ever catch you two together, I will kill him!"

I tried to reason with Craig by bringing up the point that he and I were not a couple, and we were not sleeping together.

Craig didn't care, he said that we were living together right now, and it would make him look bad if anyone found out that I was spending time with another man.

It was the evening of Father's Day and Craig decided that he wanted to talk to me. For some reason, he wanted to confess to me everything that he had ever done.

I said, "Hold on, I don't want you to admit anything to me. Everything between us is fine now, but I don't ever want there to come a time when you have to decide if you need to kill me to keep me from talking because I know too much."

Craig said, "I don't see that happening, but okay, I'll just tell you everything that I have been accused of doing."

I agreed. Craig went on to tell me about all the murders he was accused of committing. He said that he had never actually been charged with a drug crime. While I thought that was the biggest part of his troubles with the law, it seems as though drugs were just the tip of the iceberg. We sat up all night as Craig detailed each case formed against him. What stood out most to me was when Craig said that he was tired, tired of that life. He said he knew Ethan was after him, that he physically couldn't run, and he was just too tired to fight.

Monday morning, everything seemed to be back to normal.

7:50 AM - I left to take David to the babysitter and then off to work. As I pulled out of the driveway, I saw Craig leaving out of the house. He had the full cast, but it was on his left leg, so he was still able to drive. As I drove down the street, I looked back in the rearview mirror and saw him getting into his car.

8:55 AM - I arrived at work.

10:58 AM - I answered my work phone. It was my younger cousin, Toya.

"Jewels, did CJ spend the night with you and Craig last night?"

"No, why?"

"Because my friend who lives down the street from you just called me and said that there is a police car in front of your house. There is a little boy inside the police car and from the way she described him, it sounded like CJ to me."

"Well, CJ wasn't with us, so have your friend go back down there and see what's going on."

11:03 AM - I paged Craig to go back and see what was happening at the house.

11:15 AM - I answered my work phone. It was Toya again.

"Jewels, does Craig still have that cast on his leg?"

"Yes, why?"

Slowly Toya said, "Because he's lying on the side of your house... dead!"

I froze for a minute.

"Jewels, are you there?"

After another minute or so, I said, "Yeah, I'm here, let me speak to Tonya."

I was really close with Toya's mother, Tonya, and they lived nearby. I asked Tonya to go over to my house to see what was happening and that I would be there as soon as I could.

11:21 AM - Kay Elle, who had the office next to mine, happened to be walking past and heard that something was going on and stopped in my doorway as I finished talking to Craig's mother. I called and told his mom what Toya told me and asked her to meet me at the house. Kay Elle was from a neighborhood similar to Craig's and she and I had discussed Craig on many occasions. Kay Elle told me that I was in no condition to drive so she would take me home. The drive that normally took an hour seemed to me to take two hours. The whole ride home, I was trying to decide if I actually believed what I had been told. I had never experienced anything like this. Surely Toya's friend was confused. There is no way that Craig could be dead. There must be some mistake.

12:39 PM - I arrived at my house. The sidewalk was full of people, some I knew and some I had never seen. I saw a big truck that had Medical Examiner on it and a police car. I looked in the police car and sure enough, CJ was sitting in the back seat. I opened the door to check on him.

He hugged me and said, "Where's my dad, Jewels?"

"I just got here sweetie so I'm not sure. Stay here and let me go see what's going on."

"You'll come back?"

"I promise."

I kissed him on his forehead and closed the car door.

I began to walk toward my house through all the people.

I saw my Aunt Tonya who just hugged me and said, "I am so sorry."

I walked up my driveway. I saw a police officer and a detective. Behind him was Craig's car that had been pulled all the way up to the side door of the house with the driver's side and passenger's side doors open. The bay window near the side door was broken and there were holes the size of golf balls in the aluminum siding and chunks missing from several bricks on the side of the house. The screen on the house's side door was opened just enough to see Craig's keys hanging from the inside door. I looked down and saw blood, a huge pool of blood that was running into the grass and down the concrete driveway. My eyes followed the blood to a mostly covered body that was on the ground. I couldn't see the face, but the left leg was exposed. A left leg with a cast on it and Craig's all white K-Swiss tennis shoe. I was amazed that with all that blood, not one drop fell on his bright white shoe. My eyes were fixed on the body when I realized that the detective had been talking to me the whole time.

"Miss, is this your house?" he asked again.

I nodded my head, "yes".

1:00 PM - The police detective told me that he needed to speak with me in private. So, we went to the black, unmarked police car sitting across the street from my house.

The detective explained, "We believe the body to be that of Craig Goodwin. Mr. Goodwin put the keys in the lock of the side door but because the door wasn't actually open, we can't go in without your permission. We have had several dealings with Mr. Goodwin, and we are very well aware of who he is. We don't think that you have anything to do with that part of his life, and we aren't after you in any way. As long as you cooperate with us, we'll leave you alone. Now you can say no, which would mean that we would have to go downtown and get a warrant to enter your home. So, we will get in either way but if you make it easy for us, we'll make it easy for you."

He went on to ask if there were any drugs or weapons in the house.

I told him that there were no drugs and that the only weapon I knew about was probably on Craig because I didn't know him to go anywhere without it.

"What happened to him?" I asked.

"Well according to witnesses, as Mr. Goodwin turned into your driveway, another car stopped at the corner. Three men got out and jumped the fences between the corner and your house. Since the house next to you has those high hedges, they were able to hide behind them without being seen. When Mr. Goodwin exited the vehicle to enter the house, they opened fire on him with AK-47s. After the shots began, witnesses saw a female running down the street. We found this shoe on the railroad tracks."

"That must have been Donna, the mother of the little boy in the police car, CJ. She left him there?"

"There were also two babies in the back seat of Mr. Goodwin's vehicle."

"She just left all her babies and ran?"

"Looks that way," he said. The detective asked me if I knew who did this.

I said that I didn't know.

1:28 PM - Craig's mother knocked on the window of the detective's car. I rolled down the window.

"I need to know where Craig keeps his money so I can bury him."

"I don't know where the money is, he didn't keep it here."

"Well, I need something so I can pay to bury him. What about that?" she said as she pointed to the ring on my finger.

It was about three carats, and it was Craig's, I just happened to be wearing it that day. I gave it to his mother. I couldn't help but think... your son is lying on the ground dead in a pool of his own blood and all you can think about is getting your hands on his money. Craig told me that he didn't think his mother cared about him and that she was always working some angle to get money from him. It wasn't until now that I understood why he felt that way.

Before his mother walked away, she said, "Hang tough and remember the rules."

I just looked at her.

The detective repeated the question, "Do you know who did this?"

"No."

"Do you expect me to believe that you have no idea who wanted to take him out?"

"Look, as you said yourself, I didn't have anything to do with that part of his life. I understand that it exists, but I knew a totally different person. You can go in the house and do what you need to do, take what you need to take, but I can't help you with who did this. What I want to know is, why he is still lying there like that?"

The detective explained, "While the Medical Examiner has been here, he couldn't move the body until we got here to investigate the scene. We were delayed because a little girl was shot on her porch earlier."

I thought to myself, "Why is he discussing another case as if that makes it okay that Craig is still lying on the ground?"

Then I said, "Okay, can you explain why all these people are standing around here? What if the person who did it is right here? Can't you make all these people go away?"

2:04 PM - The detective and I exited the car. Craig's identification didn't, of course, say Craig Goodwin because Craig never carried anything with his real name on it. He had used several aliases throughout the years, but the one he was currently using was Curtis Grant. So the driver's license, social security card and voter's registration card that he had in his wallet all said Curtis Grant. He always picked a first name that began with C so that CJ could always be CJ. Anyway, because his ID was different from who they thought he was, the body needed to be identified. I wanted to do it.

"I understand that you want to see him but trust me, you don't. One of the bullets hit him in the cheek so there is a big hole in the side of his face. Believe me when I tell you that the pictures you want to keep in your mind are the ones that you already remember. If you see him now it will haunt you for the rest of your life. Let someone else do it."

Reluctantly, I said, "That was his mother who came to the car earlier, she can do it."

"That's a good choice. I'm still going to need you to come down to the station."

"Okay but I need to talk to CJ and make a phone call first. And you said the babies were in the car, where are they now?"

I went back to the police car, opened the door and sat inside with CJ.

He climbed on my lap and said, "Where is my dad?"

"Your dad was shot."

CJ had been through his father being shot a couple of times, so I thought he understood what that meant.

"How long will it be before he comes home?"

I looked CJ in his big hopeful eyes and said, "He's not coming home this time sweetie."

2:16 PM - I went next door to use the telephone. The phone was on one of those shelves made into the wall at the end of the hallway. I dialed 1 and 10 other digits before the phone rang three times.

Autumn answered, "Hello."

I could barely get out the words, "It's Jewels."

"What's wrong?"

I was quiet so Autumn said, "What's the matter?"

"It's Craig." I finally said.

"What's Craig? What's wrong? What happened?"

I was on the phone with Autumn but in this moment, I wasn't sure if I could actually say the words.

"Jewels, what happened to my brother?"

I softly said, "Autumn, Ethan got him, Craig's gone."

I heard the phone fall to the floor.

Then I heard Autumn at the top of her lungs say, "NOOOOOOO! NOOOOOO! NOOOOOOO!"

I slid down the side of the wall and sat on the floor. All the emotion that I had not allowed myself to feel all day rose to the surface and poured out in tears. I held the phone to my ear while Autumn and I cried.

2:41 PM - I took CJ, located the twins and made sure that they all went with Craig's mother. It was time for me to go to the police station, but the police were not finished in the house. I asked my Aunt Tonya if she would stay and make sure that the house was secure after the police finished. I also asked her if she would pick up David and told her that I would pick him up later.

3:10 PM - I walked into 1300 Beaubien, Police Headquarters. The detective took me into an office and told me that I could have a seat and he would be right with me. I looked up and who did I see but Donna.

"I can't believe you left your children in that car and just ran away."

Donna tried to explain that she was terrified and didn't think. She heard the shots, saw Craig drop to the ground, jumped out of the car and just ran. She went to the police station to report what happened and had been at the police station ever since. In my opinion, there was nothing Donna could say to justify her actions.

After a while, I couldn't deal with hearing the sound of Donna's voice anymore, so I interrupted. "By the way, not that you bothered to ask, but your children are fine. I sent them home with Craig's mother."

Then I walked away from Donna and sat back at the detective's desk.

5:55 PM - I arrived at my Aunt Tonya's house. My little three-year-old cousin, Patrick, was there. He was like my own child; we spent a lot of time together. As I walked in, Patrick said, "Hi Jewels!" I couldn't speak to Patrick or anyone else. I just went into my aunt's room and laid on the far side of the king-sized bed.

Patrick entered the room and said, "What's wrong?" I still didn't respond.

Patrick sat on the bed next to me. He stroked my hair. "It's going to be okay, Jewels."

He was so sweet, and I wanted to say something strong, but all I could do was cry.

My neighbor behind me knew my aunt, who was high up in the Detroit Police Department. He called her and told her what was going on at my house. While my aunt couldn't be bothered to check on me herself, she thought that it was serious enough to tell her brother Justice, my father.

Justice caught up with me at Tonya's house.

"What can I do?" asked Justice.

"Craig's family is pressing me to get in the house so that they can get his belongings. Tonya had to get the police to put them out yesterday because they were trying to remove whatever they thought belonged to him while I was at the police station."

"I will contact them and let them know that they will have only one opportunity to go to the house and retrieve his belongings and that we will meet them there tomorrow at 1:00 PM."

"Thanks, Dad! I'll see you tomorrow."

The next day, Justice and I were the first to arrive at my house. Justice looked around at all of the damage. In addition to the damage on the exterior of the house, the kitchen, which is right off the driveway, was shot up pretty badly. The kitchen cabinet closest to the window had bullet holes in it and the dishes inside were broken. There was a hole the size of a golf ball in the wall between the kitchen and the dining room. There was also a bullet hole going through the microwave oven.

I was afraid that Justice was going to be upset with me. Justice looked at me and said, "What did you get yourself into?"

"Dad, I did know that he was into selling drugs, but I didn't have anything to do with that part of his life. I thought that as long as I stayed out of it, that everything would be okay."

Justice, who very much grew up in the streets, said, "You can't separate these things. If you live that life, eventually it will follow you home." He added, "If you want to move, I will help you get out of here and set up someplace else."

"Thank you but no. The person that he was beefing with knows that I don't have anything to do with what was going on. So, I'm not concerned for my safety. I'm good staying here."

"Alright, well we will get these people in and out and get the house fixed back up and you can begin to move on."

"Thank you, Daddy!"

Craig's mother, sister, and Donna all showed up to the house. I showed them where Craig's clothes were. That was really all that was at my house that belonged to him. Most of his things were still at his house.

Donna and I decided to take a walk outside to talk and clear the air between us. Donna said, "Thanks for taking care of my kids the other day." Based on everything that I had heard and seen, I secretly thought that Donna felt trapped by Craig because he moved on with his life but would not allow her to move on. I also thought that Donna sold Craig out to Ethan in the hope that Ethan would kill Craig and secure her freedom. In my version of what happened, Donna knew what was coming so she jumped out of the car ahead of time. If Craig and the kids were gone, she would be completely free.

Our talk didn't change my thoughts on the events that led up to Craig's death, but I also wanted to know what Donna's problem was with me. "So, Donna, I have watched you interact with and be nice to other women who Craig was involved with. Why were you so hostile with me all the time?"

Donna responded, "I was nice to the others, but it was only because they didn't know any better. They believed him when he told them that we aren't married. If I said anything, he would tell me to prove it by showing them my wedding ring. We both know that he took my ring so I couldn't produce it. My issue with you was that you knew we were married. I didn't need to prove it to you because you already knew."

"I get that Donna. I was always confused by your situation with him and like the others, I believed his version of everything. You're right, I did know. I apologize."

As Donna and I walked and talked, we saw a car drive down the street. Driving the car was Ethan. We both saw him at the same time and took off running back to the house.

The family, including Autumn, thought that I knew where Craig's money was and just wouldn't tell them, so they told me that they weren't having a funeral. I later found out that they did have one, a private one, that I wasn't invited to attend. I was accustomed to Craig's family acting shady. I was, however, very disturbed by the fact that Autumn was going along with them. I thought Autumn and I knew each other; Autumn really didn't know me at all and clearly, I didn't know Autumn either. That was when I realized grief doesn't make people honest—it makes them territorial. I never saw or spoke with Autumn again.

After what happened to Craig, I was no longer comfortable using the side door of my house. The hedges that concealed Craig's killers were a problem for me. Christopher was visiting his mom, who lived next door, and he stopped by to check on me and to see if I needed anything. I asked him if he would be willing to cut down the hedges that sat between my house and his mom's house. He said yes and cut them down immediately which opened the line of sight in the backyard. I still wasn't using the side door, but it made me feel safer. I kept to myself and stayed in the house for a few months; I only left to go to work.

Chapter 17
Damien Lewis

Julianna...

As I pulled into the parking structure at work, I saw a guy standing outside of the parking attendant booth looking at me. I parked, went into the building, and got into the elevator to go upstairs. As I entered the elevator, I noticed that the same guy from the parking structure was already in the elevator. I couldn't figure out why he was in the elevator or how he got over there so quickly. I pushed the button to my floor and noticed that he had already pushed the button to the top floor of the building. We seemed to cross paths quite frequently over the next few weeks. He began to engage me in conversation, and we started dating.

Damien was 6'4", light-skinned with green eyes, beautiful teeth, and nice, thick lips. He was really sweet but a little on the crazy side. For example, he thought... well, I wasn't sure if he exactly thought it, but he used to say that he was a vampire. I always took it as a joke. He also said that his mother was a witch. Now I didn't believe that his mother was a witch; however, I was sure never to eat or drink anything when we visited his mom... 'cause you never know.

No one was the same all the time, but Damien seemed unaware of the changes in his personality. After a while, I started joking about his three distinct personalities, and I named them. Damien was the normal, fun personality; this was the mode that Damien was in most of the time. DJ was the shy, sweet, childlike personality. DJ was easily embarrassed and would blush at normal adult conversation. Dirk was the mean one; he was actually quite cruel. Dirk would lose his temper and really hurt people, verbally and physically. I had seen them all but the times that Dirk came out, his temper was never directed at me.

Damien used to tell me about these experiences that he had with his ex-girlfriend. He told me that they used to get caught in these alternate spiritual realms and come into contact with evil spirits. I was raised in the church, so I had been taught about God and Satan, but I had never been told about all these other spiritual dimensions that he was talking about. I was so convinced it was just a part of his act that I played along—treated the alternate realms as reality and asked him questions about them.

Damien played with the Ouija Board fairly often. All I knew about a Ouija Board was that it was in the toy stores with all the other board games, and that traditionally, Black people didn't play those types of games. Damien told me about the Ouija Board and how no one was supposed to use it alone because the bad spirits could take over your body. The other rule is that one wasn't supposed to keep it under your bed because your spirit could drain into the board. While using the board, one was never supposed to ask for physical proof that a spirit is real because it opens the gate for that spirit to cross over into the physical world. These rules seemed like a bit much to me, and I knew that Damien broke all the rules, but it was a game so what harm could really come of it?

As I pulled up to the house, I looked twice at the address Damien had given me. He lived in this old rickety house that barely had enough paint on it so that you'd know it was once white. It looked like one good storm or a serious huff and puff from a determined wolf could just blow it down. The front stairs were a safety hazard, and I had no idea how the little old lady he lived with named Elizabeth could get in or out of the house. I was never sure how Damien was related to Ms. Elizabeth, but it was just the two of them living in the house. Just standing outside of the house made me nervous. I was afraid of what I was going to see when I went in. It was bad enough that I was going into this crazy looking house on October 30, known in Detroit as Devil's Night, there was no way that I was going to be caught in there after nightfall. It would be like when I was a kid, when the streetlights came on, I had to go!

After braving the front stairs and porch, I rang the doorbell. Damien answered and I followed him into the house. I couldn't believe my eyes. The house looked like a little country inn. Nice and clean with hardwood floors and floral-printed furniture. Antique picture frames were on the walls holding faded black and white photographs that I figured were Ms. Elizabeth's loved ones who had passed on long ago. Damien led me through the house and down to a hallway with several closed doors. He opened the first door on the left and indicated with his arm that I should go in. The walls were bright red and were filled with posters of Jimi Hendrix. There were also two electric guitars mounted to the wall: one yellow and one red. The only furniture in the room was an old dresser and a queen-sized bed with no headboard or footboard.

The purpose of the visit was that I was tired of hearing about the Ouija Board and wanted to experience it for myself. Damien pulled the box out from under his bed. We sat in the middle of his room on the floor with the board between us. The board unfolded and felt like a regular game board, but it had the alphabet across it and the numbers 1 through 9 and 0 printed at the bottom. The word yes was printed above the alphabet to the left and to the right was the word no. At the bottom of the board was the word goodbye. The planchette was a heart-shaped piece of wood that's moved across the board by the spirits to deliver messages to the people touching it. Damien instructed me to lightly touch the planchette with my fingers, and he did the same. We moved it around a few times; Damien said that it was to warm up the planchette. Then he told me to ask the board a question.

I asked, "What is my grandmother's name?"

The planchette began to move and spelled out the letters S-A-R-A-H.

Now Sarah is my grandmother's name, but what had me thinking was how the board knew which grandmother I was referring to. Then the planchette began to move again and spelled out the letters...

C-U-R-T-I-S.

I quickly removed my hands from the planchette. Damien asked what that was, and I told him that it was the answer to the question I was thinking—what was my uncle's name.

After a couple of minutes of reflecting, I determined that I had to be the one moving the planchette. Damien didn't know my grandmother's name and he certainly didn't know the question that I was thinking, so it had to be me. I was determined not to further influence the process in any way. Damien asked a couple of questions and the planchette didn't move. Damien explained to me that sometimes he gets repeat spirits so I should ask the name of the spirit who was present.

"Who are you?"

The planchette spelled out the letters C-R-A-I-G.

I froze for a minute. "Craig who?"

The letters G-O-O-D-W-I-N were then spelled out.

Craig Goodwin. Now my head was all messed up. Damien asked who Craig Goodwin was, but I didn't respond. I hadn't discussed with Damien or anyone else who wasn't involved at the time, what happened, and I wasn't about to start now.

I took a deep breath, exhaled, and put my fingers back on the planchette.

I asked the spirit who called himself Craig Goodwin, "Where are you?"

H-E-L-L

"What is it like there?"

S-A-M-E

"The same as here?"

The planchette moved to the word YES. "Did someone set you up to be killed?" The planchette moved to the word YES.

"Who?"

A-U-T-U-M-N

I was not prepared for that response. And that answer is what convinced me that it wasn't me moving the planchette subconsciously. I did believe that Craig was set up, but I always thought that it was Donna.

Autumn was my girl. Even with the things that Autumn had said in the past, I never even considered that she set her brother up to be killed.

I flashed back to the day that Autumn joked about turning Craig in when he was on the Michigan's Most Wanted list. I also flashed back to the drug deal-gone-bad where Autumn's boyfriend disappeared with Craig's money.

"Is there anything that you want to tell me?"

C-O-M-E, there was a slight pause...

B-A-C-K

"Come back, where... to the board again?"

The planchette moved to the word YES.

"Okay, is there anything else you want to tell me?"

W-A-T-C-H O-U-T

"For what?"

H-I-M

"Who, Damien?"

The planchette moved to the word YES.

Damien's fingers were still on the planchette, but I was so involved in this conversation that I had forgotten that he was there.

"Watch out for Damien?" I said.

"Why? Is he going to hurt me physically?"

The planchette moved to the word NO.

"How then?"

S-O-U-L

"Soul, he's after my soul?"

The planchette moved to the word YES.

I looked up at Damien and asked him if it was true.

Damien nodded his head and said, "Yes, it's true."

There wasn't much left to say after that, so I excused myself and left. As I drove home, I kept replaying in my mind what had just happened. I really needed to talk to Lisa.

Chapter 18
Monster's Ball

Julianna came from a very spiritual family. Both Lisa and India were what Julianna referred to as "sold out for Jesus." Julianna grew up studying with her sisters and she was aware of the spiritual gifts that she possessed. Lisa was the oldest and the most versed in what they called all things spiritual.

The family dynamic seemed to be fairly normal. Everyone got along and interacted as necessary. India looked mostly to Julianna for her advice and spent her time away at the University of Michigan dispensing it to her friends as her own. Julianna loved India and enjoyed being a big sister, but Julianna loved being a little sister too. She adored her big sister. India would tell anyone who would listen; "Big sisters are great, and everyone should have one!" It was an opinion that Julianna shared.

Julianna knew that Lisa was technically India's big sister too, but she felt like India had a big sister so Lisa was hers. Julianna looked up to Lisa, wanted her approval and feared her disapproval more than that of their parents.

Lisa did not approve of Julianna dating Craig, so Julianna stopped talking about him and led Lisa to believe that she wasn't seeing him any longer. And because she did that, she didn't feel as though she could tell Lisa when Craig was killed. While Damien was not living the life that Craig was, he certainly challenged most, if not all the spiritual beliefs of the family. Anytime Julianna brought up Lisa, Damien would get all pissed off and tell her not to discuss him with Lisa. Since Julianna couldn't give Lisa all the standard details, it was just easier not to talk about Damien either. Lisa was really on Julianna about her spiritual journey because she knew something was going on with Julianna and Julianna wasn't talking about it. Lisa had spiritual gifts that allowed her to see things, mostly through dreams. If Lisa told you she had a dream about you, it was pretty much a lock that whatever she saw was going to happen. Unbeknownst to Julianna, Lisa had been having dreams about her. She was being warned that Julianna was in trouble. Fortunately for Julianna, Lisa prayed and prayed for her and then prayed some more. If she had a particularly bad dream, she would wake Michael up and ask him to pray too. Lisa interceded on Julianna's behalf so regularly during that time that to this day, they believe that is what saved Julianna.

Julianna had been struggling with the events that occurred during her visit with Damien. Should she believe everything that she heard from the Ouija Board? How was one supposed to take it when a spirit came from hell to warn you about someone you knew? And wouldn't someone who wasn't after her soul deny the accusation? She had been avoiding Damien for two weeks, which wasn't easy since he was always popping up when she least expected it. Damien called and wanted to visit, so Julianna told him that he could. When he went into the house, he went straight to Julianna's bedroom. Yes, they had been seeing each other for a while but they weren't having sex, and they didn't hang out in Julianna's bedroom, so she was confused as to why he went in there. She followed him into the room, watched him sit on the edge of her bed and asked him what was up.

"I've been thinking about what happened, and I know that you are unsure about some things. If you just let me reveal to you my true self, I'm sure it will answer all of your questions."

"Okay, go ahead."

Julianna's eyes went up to the ceiling when the lights inexplicably went out. She looked back at Damien and screamed at the top of her lungs. With only the moonlight that seeped in through the window for light, Julianna could see that his head and neck had turned red and leather-like, and every vein he had was protruding. He had no hair, and his forehead was wrinkled like that of a Klingon and hung over his deeply sunken yellow cat eyes. His nostrils were extremely oversized; the tip of his nose was long and pointed. His cheekbones were high and went right into his ears, which were long, hollow and pointed. Black gums surrounded his rotting vampire-like teeth and his chin stretched to be three inches long and was square. His neck was twice the normal size, and she could see the muscles that connected his neck to his head stretching the skin to the point where it looked like it was about to rip open.

Julianna could feel her heart beating in her throat as she said, "YOU NEED TO GET OUT!"

The beast that was Damien only moments before stood up, his voice was heavy and sounded more like a roar.

"SO, WHAT, DO YOU THINK YOU'RE JUST GOING TO PUT ME OUT?"

"Look, Damien or Dirk or whoever or whatever you are right now, you need to leave."

Damien walked up on her. "IS THAT RIGHT?"

His giant red hand grabbed her by her throat and threw her up against the wall. Julianna could no longer feel the floor underneath her feet, but she felt pain in the back of her head so strong that it made her face hurt. She was dizzy for just a few seconds before her body went limp in Damien's hand. Damien slowly moved Julianna's hair from her face, kissed her on the mouth, opened his hand and smiled as he watched her fall to the floor.

Julianna woke up the next morning to the voices of Lisa and India begging her to wake up.

When Julianna opened her eyes, Lisa said, "What happened? When we got here the door was wide open."

India was crying, "Who did this to you?"

Julianna closed her eyes and held her head to try and make the pain go away. She was lying on the bed but didn't remember how she got there. Her clothes had been torn off. She could taste the blood from her busted lip. She could feel the sting from the scratches across her neck and chest and her private parts no longer felt private. "Why are you here?"

Lisa said, "You never picked up David last night, and you haven't been answering your phone. I called India and she hadn't heard from you either, so we came over. Are you okay?"

"I'm not sure."

Julianna felt herself drift off to sleep as the sound of sirens got closer and closer.

When Julianna woke up again, she was at the hospital. Lisa and India were there as well. Lisa was no longer willing to accept Julianna's evasive answers to what had been going on in her life. Julianna explained to her sisters what happened with Damien and because that explanation wouldn't make sense without the information regarding Craig, Julianna told them everything that happened with him too.

Part Five:

The Lie

Chapter 19
Love Jones

It had been nearly two years since the night with Damien. With Lisa and India beside her, Julianna had done the work of putting herself back together—slowly, quietly, and on her own terms.

There was a meeting being held in Julianna's department. Attending were staff members from various departments of the hospital as well as some outside guests. Julianna happened to be in the lobby when the two-hour meeting was over. A man walked up to her and asked if there was a telephone that he could use. She said sure and showed him to the phone in the office next to hers. She pretended to go back to work, but all she was working on was checking him out. He was extremely good-looking and impeccably dressed, 6'1" with a medium build, and had a beautiful smile. He had the same caramel-colored skin as Julianna, a great voice, and no wedding ring. He was very professional but with an edge... the way he talked to her was really smooth. He used the phone, said thank you and left.

Kay Elle stopped in Julianna's office, and they were having their daily catch-up session when Richard, one of the research scientists from Research and Development, came into the department. Julianna's department handled all aspects of getting money into the hospital, Julianna's focus was on conducting special events to raise money. Julianna heard Richard introducing a new hire. She hated when new people started, just somebody else that she had to break in and get them to understand that she did things her way.

When Richard entered Julianna's office, she and Kay Elle were still talking.

"Hey Julianna and Kay Elle, this is Dave Alexander, he's the new AIDS Research Scientist."

Julianna and Kay Elle looked at him, looked at each other and then looked at him again. It was that fine guy from a few months before who asked to use the telephone. He went over and shook both Julianna's and Kay Elle's hands as Richard explained their functions within the department. Julianna knew she had to be smiling hard because Richard just stared at her. After Julianna told Dr. David Alexander that she was pleased to meet him, he turned and walked out.

When Richard looked back at Julianna she whispered, "What's up with him?"

He gestured with his fingers like he was sliding a ring on his left ring finger and mouthed, "He's married."

Damn… oh well!

Julianna needed to go to Research and Development to deliver a report. She entered the office, and the only person she saw was Dave. He jumped up and went right over to her, stating that he was just on his way over to see her. Oh really, she thought. He informed her that he needed to plan an event and that he was told that she was the person who could make it happen. His event didn't have anything to do with work; it was a huge celebration for his parents so this would be a personal favor that needed to be planned outside of work. Julianna agreed to meet with him to discuss the details. When he turned around to get his datebook, Julianna noticed that he wasn't wearing his lab coat, and that she liked the view from the back just as much as from the front. She loved the way his sweater laid over his back and shoulders, not to mention the fact that his butt looked great in his slacks. Julianna left him with her telephone number. They met several times to begin laying out the details of the event. Each time they met, they handled the business they needed to discuss then they hung out for a while just getting to know each other.

Julianna was on her way to the cafeteria on a break and saw Damien.

"Hey Jewels, what's going on?"

Julianna froze for a minute then ran into the cafeteria right into the arms of Dave. He held her and asked what was wrong. Julianna slowly looked up, saw his face, smelled his cologne, and felt his arms around her. For the first time in a long time, she felt safe and said that nothing was wrong. He released her and they chatted for a while, during which time Julianna was trying to ascertain whether Dave was flirting with her or if it was just wishful thinking on her part. She didn't usually have an issue with identifying the flirt, but she was trippin' because unlike the first time she saw him, he was wearing a wedding ring.

Julianna had a habit of licking her lips. She saw him notice it, but when he actually commented, she knew for sure that he was flirting. And Julianna liked it! He told Julianna that she had better think about whether she wanted to mess with him or not.

Julianna quickly responded with, "No! You'd better think about whether you want to mess with me or not."

They both laughed. When Julianna went to leave the cafeteria, she remembered Damien was out there, so she waited for Dave and went in the elevator with him.

Their next meeting was at Julianna's house. She had out all the work they had completed to date and was ready to review. Their conversation was very personal this time. Somehow, Dave was under the impression that Julianna had a boyfriend. He thought that would be cool considering his situation and would keep Julianna from getting too attached. However, finding out that she wasn't seeing anyone didn't seem to make a difference.

Julianna asked what was up with his situation. Why wasn't he wearing his wedding ring when she first saw him? He explained that the first time they saw each other he and his wife, Quintella, were separated. He came from a good family but got caught up in the street life as a teenager. They met, fell in love, and got married while they were young. Dave decided that he no longer wanted to live that life. He received good grades effortlessly in high school. So, when he was ready to go to college, it was easy. He began to change his life, but Quintella liked the fast life. The marriage had broken up, they separated, and then she was diagnosed with leukemia. Before her treatment began, he went back home. With the anticancer drug treatment, the five-year survival rate was 90%. They weren't quite back together, but he didn't want her to have to deal with the cancer alone. They hadn't made it to the physical recovery part yet, so they hadn't consummated the reunion.

Julianna could hear Janet Jackson singing *Funny How Times Flies* in the background. They never worked on the event that night.

Everyone called him Dave, but Julianna never cared for that nickname. Since her son's name was David too, she didn't want to call him that either. When she introduced him or discussed him with other people, she used Dr. Alexander. When she addressed him directly, she called him Alex. They were inseparable. They were together six to seven days a week, every week. They spent as much time together at work as possible. They took their breaks and lunches together every day, and he visited her office all the time as well. Months passed and they were as hot and heavy as ever.

Before Alex arrived, Julianna took her breaks and lunches with Kay Elle. So, it was obvious to Kay Elle that something was going on between Julianna and Alex. One day, Alex was visiting Julianna in her office. Kay Elle was walking by, saw him in there and decided to test her theory and go in. She walked in, sat down, said, "Hey, what are we talking about?" and looked back and forth at Julianna and Alex with a big grin on her face.

Alex said, "Hello."

Julianna said, "Hey Kay, don't you have a meeting to prep for?"

"Nope, I'm ready!" said Kay Elle.

"Okay, well do you need something?"

"No, I just came to hang out."

"Well, I was in the middle of a conversation with Dr. Alexander."

"Oh, I don't mind waiting. Go ahead."

"Kay!"

Kay Elle was acting like an annoying little sister, and she knew exactly what she was doing. She laughed to herself as she got up and left Julianna's office.

Alex was everything Julianna wanted and more. One might think that the marriage thing would have been an issue, but it so wasn't. Emotionally, Julianna had her walls up to protect her heart. She allowed herself to love Anthony and he hurt her and left her. Even now, he's in her life but not for real. She's terrified that she'll get the word that he didn't make it out of some battle of some war that he's fighting in some other country. Julianna even let Dean in and look how that turned out. Clearly this relationship with Alex could only go so far. She was free to be in the moment with him. She didn't worry about the future; she just enjoyed the present. She loved him, and he loved her, and that's all they dealt with. The outside world didn't matter when they were together... it was just them. It was a low-risk situation for her, and they were great together in every way. They talked about any and everything and dated very openly. He was at her house all the time. They went out to lunch, out to dinner, the clubs, wherever... whenever. He stayed all night whenever she wanted. Julianna's friends and family all knew him and knew he was her man. She never let them in on the married part, but they knew the rest. She saw him on most holidays, and he even introduced her to his parents.

His wife was an issue from time to time, for Alex not for Julianna. Quintella and Julianna crossed paths once. By the time that happened, Quintella already knew that he was seeing someone, she just didn't know who. Julianna stopped by Alex's lab to let him know that she was leaving work early. Alex let her know that Quintella was on her way and Julianna was not happy about it. Julianna told Alex that she didn't go into Quintella's territory, and she didn't want Quintella in hers. Julianna's back was to the door and as she and Alex continued to talk, he looked towards the door. Julianna turned around to see Quintella standing there. Clearly, he had no choice but to introduce the two of them. Alex did, but you could cut the tension with a knife. After about forty-five seconds, Julianna excused herself and left.

Alex visited Julianna at her home later that day, as usual, and told her that Quintella knew Julianna was the person he had been seeing. Julianna asked how she knew. She told him that she knew what he liked, which was interesting to Julianna because Quintella and Julianna looked nothing alike.

By the time the celebration for his parents came around, Alex was in love with Julianna and she with him.

Alex told Julianna that Quintella made comments like, "What excuse are you going to use to see your girlfriend now that the event is over?"

He did what he had to do and said what he had to say to spend time with Julianna. She didn't care too much about his home drama; it just made him want to spend more time with her.

It was Julianna's birthday the following year and Alex wanted to take her out. He wouldn't tell her where they were going; he just said that it was a surprise and that she would like it. Alex picked Julianna up, and they drove toward downtown Detroit. As they came off I-75 and drove east down Jefferson, Julianna had no idea where they were going. They soon pulled up to a Japanese restaurant named Hoi Tin. When Julianna was little, her family dined there, and she loved it. In Japanese culture, the proper way of sitting during a meal is to kneel (seiza). Since most Americans can't kneel for more than a few minutes, Hoi Tin had openings beneath each of the tables so that guests could actually sit at the low tables and still have room for their legs.

Julianna hadn't been there in many years and was excited that he remembered the story she shared with him. She had forgotten that she even told Alex about it. Taking her to that restaurant was one of the most thoughtful things that any man had ever done for her. They had such a great time. The restaurant was just as Julianna remembered. The food, all seven courses, and the conversation were phenomenal. They realized that as much as they talked, there were still some subjects they hadn't discussed before.

Chapter 20
Fade to Black

Alex was describing his sexual fantasy for Julianna. Like many men, his fantasy was to have a threesome with two women. Julianna was willing to do many things for Alex but watching him have sex with another woman was definitely where she drew the line. She knew that she couldn't handle it and she wasn't willing to try. He kept bringing the conversation back up, trying to find a way to make it work. Finally, Alex suggested that instead of another woman, they try it with another man. Julianna did find that she was a little more interested in that scenario. The conversation moved to who the other guy would be. Over a period of a couple of weeks, Alex suggested a few people, all of whom Julianna opposed. Her theory was that if it wasn't someone who she would be interested in on her own, he wasn't going to get a free pass because Alex walked him in the door.

Julianna thought that maybe since they hadn't come to an agreement that Alex would let this idea go. She also thought that his real motivation behind letting the guy come in was so that she would feel obligated to return the favor. She kept insisting that it wouldn't happen, but she still believed Alex thought he could talk her into it. Knowing how she felt about the possibility of watching Alex with someone else, she asked Alex how he could be okay watching her be with someone else. He told her that it was a guy thing. He knew it wouldn't mean anything to her, so it wouldn't bother him.

One day, Alex told Julianna about a friend of his from school named Lorenzo Black. Alex and Lorenzo had been cool since the days before Alex decided to stop living like a gangster and continue his education. Alex told Julianna that when they were younger, Alex stayed in so much trouble that when he got home from college people were asking him when he got out (of prison).

Lorenzo was in Alex's wedding and according to Alex, Lorenzo was about to get married, and Alex was going to be in his wedding. Julianna had never met Lorenzo, but clearly, Alex was ready for them to meet. Alex assured Julianna that she would like Lorenzo because all the girls in school loved him. Julianna wasn't convinced but she was willing to meet him with the understanding that if she wasn't feeling him, she could put on the brakes.

It was Friday night. Dean's mother came by earlier and picked David up for the weekend. Julianna poured herself a drink while she waited for Alex and Lorenzo to arrive. Halfway through her drink, the doorbell rang. Julianna hurried to finish her drink, and then answered the door. Alex greeted her with a kiss and a hug and introduced her to Lorenzo. Julianna and Lorenzo exchanged pleasantries and checked each other out. Lorenzo was about 5'10" with skin that was the color of deep dark chocolate. He had a bald head, thick lips, beautiful white teeth, and visible tattoos. He had a mellow voice and was very well spoken which was especially shocking because he looked like a thug. He wasn't what would be described as traditionally good-looking, but one thing was for sure—Lorenzo had serious swag and Julianna felt the attraction immediately.

Julianna went into the den where Alex was waiting with more drinks. Lorenzo sat on the couch while Alex sat on the floor against the far wall. Alex called Julianna over to him. As she stood in front of him with her back to Lorenzo, Alex pulled the tie on her ivory robe. When the robe fell open, Alex kissed her thigh and turned her around to Lorenzo revealing the ivory lace bra and panties that she was wearing against her caramel colored skin.

Alex said to Lorenzo, "Look at all of this" and stood up.

He began kissing Julianna, and he pulled the robe from her body, and it fell to the floor.

As Alex started to undress, he turned Julianna back around to Lorenzo who said, "Well damn, why am I the only one still dressed?"

Lorenzo walked up to Julianna, came face to face with her, placed his hands on her hips and pressed his lips against hers.

Just in case everything worked out, Julianna wanted to make sure that she would be protected, so she put together a tray with an assortment of condoms. By the time the night ended, the tray was half empty. Julianna enjoyed both of them without the two of them coming into actual contact with each other.

At one point Alex got up and left the room to go to the bathroom. Lorenzo's arm hit the entertainment center, and a picture fell off the side and headed straight for their heads. When Julianna saw it coming toward them, she screamed while pushing Lorenzo's head one way and jerking hers the other. The picture fell right between their heads. Alex heard the scream, and when he came back in the room, Lorenzo and Julianna were laughing. He asked what was up and Julianna explained how the picture of her father almost hit them.

Alex and Julianna walked Lorenzo to the door. Lorenzo said goodbye and left Julianna with one final kiss. Alex and Julianna took a shower together so that Alex could have some alone time with her and make sure she was okay physically and emotionally. Alex hugged and kissed Julianna and said that he would see her the following day.

Alex visited Julianna the next day and the day after that. They went back to work on Monday, and Alex resumed trying to convince Julianna to have the threesome with another woman. The conversation continued over the next few months. Julianna had not changed her mind and she was getting irritated that he wouldn't let it go. To smooth things over with Julianna, Alex promised her that they would get to spend some real uninterrupted time together over the holiday.

Chapter 21
Happy New Year

Alex was born on New Year's Eve. It was fast approaching, and he let Julianna know that he wanted to spend it with her. He said that Quintella had been giving him grief as usual for all the time he had been spending with Julianna, and he needed a break. He planned to be at Julianna's house from December 30 to January 2. That was his plan, but Julianna had a different plan. David had been with Dean since the day after Christmas and wasn't due back until January 3, so the timing was perfect. Alex arrived at her house at 7:00 PM on December 30. They spent a quiet evening talking and watching movies. Julianna noticed that the clock read

12:01 AM, and she wished Alex happy birthday just before they drifted off to sleep. Julianna woke him up with breakfast in bed… a tray filled with Belgian waffles, turkey sausage, and a mixture of fresh cantaloupe and honeydew melon. After breakfast, Julianna told him to pack his bag because they were leaving. Alex asked where they were going but Julianna simply said that it was a surprise.

Julianna drove them to the airport, and they boarded a plane. After much delay, thanks to the unpredictable Michigan weather, they arrived safely in Toronto, Canada. They took a cab downtown to the corner of Avenue Road and Bloor Street. Despite the wall-to-wall people, as they entered the Park Hyatt Toronto, they were able to appreciate the marble floors and tall pillars that led to the check-in desk. They rode the south tower elevator to the tenth floor. Behind the door was the most beautiful 300-square-foot suite. Everything was cream and champagne in color and very plush. The bed was king-sized and had dark wood posts at the foot and a headboard that almost reached the ceiling. Robes and slippers were waiting in the bathroom, and the tub and shower area was definitely big enough to comfortably accommodate two. They had just enough time to make their appointment for their couples massage at the Stillwater Spa before enjoying a nice seafood dinner.

When they were getting dressed for the evening, Alex figured that they were going to one of the many New Year's Eve parties that were happening in the hotel or one of the other locations downtown. When they got downstairs, Julianna directed Alex to the car service that waited outside. They rode through the theatre district. They had been having a great day and were laughing and talking along the way. As the car turned the corner, they were stopped by the traffic. Alex looked out the window and noticed the *Pantages Theatre* that was built specifically for the Phantom of the Opera.

"Oh, we have to come back one day and come here, I have always wanted to see this play."

"I know you have."

Just then the traffic began to move slowly. They were directly in front of the theatre when Julianna told the driver that it was fine to let them out. Julianna led Alex into the beautiful *Pantages Theatre*. An usher took their tickets and escorted them down to the front of the theatre where they were seated in the center aisle of the fifth row.

The play was wonderful, and Alex could not believe that Julianna surprised him like that. He had no idea about any of it.

Nine months later, on October 5, Julianna gave birth to Arianna Alexander; they call her Lexi. On December 30 of the following year, Jeffrey Alexander was born; they call him Zander. Alex was present for each birth and was very attached to the babies. He stayed over more and more, and Quintella's grief about it was getting worse.

Chapter 22
Oh No She Didn't

Julianna always somewhat wanted Alex's wife, Quintella, to show up on her doorstep demanding that she leave Alex alone so Julianna could let her know exactly how she felt about everything. Quintella gave Alex the blues about her, but she never messed with Julianna. Their situation was such that Julianna knew she came first, and Quintella knew that Julianna came first. All those years, that was just the way it was. It would have stayed that way too, if only one thing had gone differently. If Alex had only known Quintella had a cousin who lived down the street from Julianna; if the cousin had just lived one street over; if Quintella hadn't upset the cousin; if the cousin hadn't tried to hurt Quintella and kept her mouth shut; if Quintella hadn't acted on what she heard. The day it happened, Julianna didn't act at all the way she thought she would.

Alex and Quintella had two cars, one that he primarily drove and one that Quintella drove.

Alex told Julianna that Quintella had a disagreement with one of her cousins. Quintella said something that upset her cousin, and the cousin fired back, "I didn't know that you knew Julianna."

When she inquired as to what the cousin was talking about, the cousin said, "I see your car down at her house every day."

The cousin knew that it was Alex's car and was just ready to start some mess. And that she did. Now Quintella not only knew who Julianna was, she knew that Alex was still seeing her, and she knew where Julianna lived. Alex parked behind the house for about two days. Then when everything seemed to go back to normal, he went back to parking out front.

It was July 4th, and Julianna and Alex planned to barbecue. As Julianna opened the door to let Alex in, she realized that he was not alone. He introduced her to his companion Quinn and explained that it was his brother-in-law. Julianna said okay but didn't really know how she was supposed to act or why he would have brought his wife's brother to her home.

He said, "Oh he's cool, don't worry about it," kissed Julianna and went into the house.

Quinn followed him in and spent the rest of the day with them.

Later that evening the doorbell rang. As Alex opened the door, Arianna ran to the door, grabbed his leg and said, "Who is it Daddy?" causing him to look down at her.

When Alex turned to see who it was, he was looking right into Quintella's face.

"Oh shit!" spilled out of his mouth without permission.

"Did she just call you Daddy?"

"Lexi, go back into the room with David and Zander. Tell Mommy I'll be right back."

He walked out and shut the door behind him.

Only Quintella knew what her intentions were when she showed up at Julianna's house that day. One thing is certain though, she got much more than she expected.

Julianna was sitting in the family room with the children watching a movie. When Alex returned, Quintella was with him. Julianna was more confused than when Quinn walked through the door. Quinn must have slipped out of the side door when Alex and Quintella came through the front door, because he was nowhere to be found.

They entered the family room and Alex said to Quintella, "I'm sure you remember Julianna."

Quintella and Julianna just looked at each other, and Julianna said, "Alex, what's going on?"

He continued, "This is our daughter Arianna, she's almost two. Julianna is holding our son Jeffrey, he's six months and the oldest is David."

Arianna smiled showing all her front teeth, waved and said, "Hi!"

David said hello and continued watching the movie. Quintella looked as if she was getting ready to fall out but she didn't say one word. Her eyes filled with tears, and she just kept shaking her head as she turned and walked out of the house.

Alex followed her out, ignoring Arianna's repeated, "Who is it, Daddy?"

Julianna put the baby in his crib and went into the living room.

Alex came back in the house, sat next to Julianna on the couch, laid his head in her lap and didn't say anything, neither did she. He stayed with Julianna that night.

It had been about a week since Quintella showed up at Julianna's house. They went back to work the next day and Alex continued to visit daily. Nothing changed. Nothing except the questions about Lorenzo. They became more frequent and more intense.

Alex kept asking, "What did Lorenzo do to you that had you screaming?"

"I keep telling you, that the picture fell off the entertainment center and almost hit us in the head."

"Yeah right!"

No matter how many times Julianna explained it, Alex didn't believe her.

Julianna hadn't seen or talked to Lorenzo since that night three years ago. Every so often the questioning began, and Julianna figured it was just time to go through it again. Inviting Lorenzo into their relationship damaged something that neither of them knew how to repair. One thing was for sure, Julianna vowed never to make that mistake again.

From that time on, anytime the subject came up with any of Julianna's friends, she always gave the same advice, "If you ever choose to have a threesome... you be the third person, never invite another person into your relationship."

This was the first time Alex and Julianna discussed his home situation since the events of the fourth. Alex began to tell Julianna what happened, "When I went back home the next day, she still wasn't speaking to me. The next two days she just cried." He paused. "By the fourth day, all hell broke loose."

Quintella said, "I knew you were seeing someone, but I thought that it was just one of your little flings. I can't believe you've been with her all this time, and you were over there having FUCKIN' babies with her. After everything you've already put me through... BABIES!? You wouldn't have babies with me, but you had them with her? Oh, hell naw, I'm taking the house and anything else I can get my hands on. You want to be over there with your BITCH and your little BASTARD kids, go right ahead but there won't be anything left for them because I'm taking it all. You will pay for this, believe it! And then what? You thought it would be better if you said FUCK me and stayed out all night when you knew I knew what was going on? Or did you just think that it was more important to stay and make sure that she was okay. Oh, don't you even worry about it. That was the last time you'll ever pick another BITCH over me!"

Alex told Julianna that while they did have children together, he was married to Quintella. He was hoping that he would never have to choose between them, but Quintella was still struggling with her leukemia, and he wouldn't leave her. Then it came out—Alex had been having sex with Quintella the entire time. Julianna knew Alex was married to Quintella, but he led Julianna to believe that she was the only one he was sleeping with. Julianna's heart sank. She felt empty and the emptiness soon began to fill with anger. Now, as crazy as it may sound, Julianna was absolutely pissed off. Right or wrong, Julianna felt betrayed.

Alex asked Julianna, "How could you think I wasn't sleeping with my own wife?"

"WOW… really, four years, two babies and everything we've been through, this is how you want to play me? Okay!"

A few months passed of Alex trying to backpedal and get back on good terms with Julianna. He didn't believe it, but Julianna was done with him. He could visit the children but quality time with her was over.

Part Six:

Lust

Chapter 23
David Alexander

Alex…

As soon as I handed Lorenzo the phone, I had a sinking feeling that I should never have even called Julianna for him. They talked for a minute before he pulled out a pen and some paper. He wrote something on the paper, put the paper in his pocket and handed me my phone back. Then he sat down and picked up the Courvoisier he ordered, with this smile on his face that just pissed me off. I know good and well that she didn't give him her number. Did she?

I was cool, though, when I talked to Lorenzo, "So what's up?"

"It's good man, we're goin' to hook up tomorrow. Good lookin' out."

What? They're going to hook up tomorrow? What in the hell is that supposed to mean? I felt sick to my stomach. I threw the rest of my Hennessy down my throat and left.

I went over to see Julianna and the babies two days later. Julianna was going off from the minute I walked in the door.

"I saw Lorenzo yesterday!"

"You what?"

"Yeah, I saw him, and I asked him what you told him about us before he and I met. He said that you didn't really say anything. You just played it like I was just some chick you knew. You didn't tell him that I was your girl, that we were together, nothing. And when you saw him the other day, you seemed to forget to mention that we had two children together. You just played me like I was some bitch off the street! If you were so concerned with keeping your life with Quintella separate from your life with me, you should never have introduced us."

What the hell? Lorenzo is supposed to be my boy. Why did he tell her all that stuff? I knew I shouldn't have trusted him. Regardless of how I said I felt about her, he should have kept his mouth shut. Okay, even if I did say that then, clearly there was more going on because she has my children now. I see that it is every man for their damn self. I see how he's laying. This just keeps getting worse and worse.

I don't know what to do about this, Julianna is actually dating Lorenzo. She has him around my babies and everything. He's out stealing cars, smoking weed and who knows what else. I don't want any of his mess to come back to hurt my babies in any way. This is messed up. I love her, but I can't believe she is doing this

to me. I get that she's mad but she's pushing me too far.
I only called Julianna that night because I wanted to
prove to Lorenzo that she wasn't interested in him... this
was NOT supposed to happen.

Chapter 24
Lorenzo Black

Lorenzo…

When I ran into Dave at the bar, I knew it was time for me to get back with Julianna. I would have gone around him if I could have, but I needed him to make contact for me. I had been having flashbacks about that night with Julianna since it happened. I couldn't get Julianna out of my head, but I didn't know how to get in touch with her. I never had her number, I didn't even know her last name, and I didn't remember exactly where her house was, or I would have just rolled up on her. When we hooked up that one time, I thought Julianna was hot. I figured that if he could talk her into doing that, there's no telling what I could talk her into doing. Yeah, I got married after that, but it's three years later and I'm not married anymore. I don't see any reason why we can't get this thing started again. Dave was acting like it wasn't a big deal to him, but I still had to press him to get him to make the call. And Julianna proved that she wanted me when I didn't have to work hard to get her number. She was giving it up as quickly as I could ask for it.

I wanted to get with her ASAP, so I called her first thing the next morning. She didn't even make me wait long. I was over there that same afternoon. When I got there, we just talked a lot at first. She was quizzing me about what Dave told me about her. He's my boy and everything, but whatever. He said there was nothing to it, so why would he care. She told me that two of her kids were Dave's... Daaaamn! She told me about the day Quintella found out; how he told her he needed to concentrate on Quintella and his marriage. I don't know what he was over there doing, but he really mind-fucked her. She is pissed and I can use that to my advantage. I told her what she wanted to know because I knew it would help me get what I wanted. He'll be alright, he needs to go home to his wife anyway.

At first, I just wanted to hit it from time to time. But the more we talked, the more time we spent together, and the more I got to know her, the more I was feeling her. It got to the point where I would do anything for her and her kids. I enjoyed being around them, and I would have loved to have that family life.

Chapter 25
Julianna Jeffries

Julianna...

I can't believe that Alex called me with Lorenzo right there. As jacked up as our situation was, how could he be out showboating about how he had me on lock? Hooking up with Lorenzo and letting him know about it should make him hurt the same way he made me hurt. And since it's not like being with Lorenzo again would be some great sacrifice on my part, I was more than happy to arrange a date to see him when Alex put him on the phone.

At 9:00 AM the next morning, Lorenzo called me. The children had spent the night over Lisa's and weren't scheduled home until after 8:00 PM. So, I told him to come over to my house at noon. I was really torn between loving Alex and wanting him to pay. My doorbell rang at 11:59 AM. At first, we just talked and got to know each other. We discussed his marriage, which ended six months after it began. We discussed my relationship with Alex and his friendship with Alex. Most importantly, I wanted to find out what he knew that I didn't. Lorenzo told me things about Alex and Quintella that I am certain that Alex didn't want me to know.

And then, when I asked him what Alex told him about me, he said that Alex led him to believe that I was just some chick that he was kickin' it with; that I didn't mean anything to him. Oh, why did he tell me that? Now I was livid, and any doubts I had about my plan for revenge went right out of the window. We moved out of the talking phase of the visit, right into the sex phase. It was different from the first time we were together. Maybe it was different because this time it was personal or maybe just because it was only us this time. He was very good in bed but definitely not better than Alex. What was enjoyable about him was that he was really into kissing. I'm a big kisser and Alex isn't that was something that I had been missing, so it was nice.

We talked more, just about my life, his life, and life in general. We had lunch, talked more, had more sex, and had dinner, had more sex, talked a little more, and then he left. He was a really cool person and I enjoyed spending time with him. When he left, it took about five minutes for me to remember what he told me Alex said and I went right back to being pissed.

In the middle of all this madness, Anthony came to see me. We still talked regularly, so he knew what was going on in my life. He realized that I had moved him into the friend zone, and he kept reminding me that was not where he wanted to be. He told me that he was thinking about marrying the girl that he had been seeing from Los Angeles. He would only do it, however, if he couldn't have me back.

I told him that I wanted him to be happy and that if he thought that he could be happy with her then he should marry her. I would always love Anthony, but I just had too much going on to be trying to figure out how to fit him into the equation.

The next day, Alex came over to see the children, and I went straight to him with everything Lorenzo told me. Things between Alex and me went from bad to worse and Alex and Lorenzo never spoke again.

I continued to see Lorenzo over the course of the next eight months. We got along really well and enjoyed each other's company. We went from seeing each other every few weeks to seeing each other three or four times a week. I really liked Lorenzo and he served a purpose in my life, as I suppose I did in his, but it wasn't anything that was going to lead to something bigger. What I liked most about Lorenzo was that he would do anything for me. If I needed anything, he would get it for me. Now, he might very well go and knock somebody over their head to get it for me, but he wouldn't come back without it. Not to mention that Lorenzo could cook. I love lobster and Lorenzo served up the best lobster in town... believe that! Lorenzo spoiled me and I enjoyed it but I was still in love with Alex. Lorenzo was my escape; I didn't have to think, all I had to do was feel good. It was what it was... no more, no less.

Alex was still seeing the children, but we made it a point to have as few words as possible. One day when I was on the freeway, it really hit me how badly I was hurting him. Our cars were right next to each other; we looked at each other and he didn't speak or wave or anything; he just looked at me with disgust and turned away. I know I said that I wanted him to hurt, but I couldn't take being the reason for his pain any longer. From that day forward, I never did anything out of revenge again.

I told Lorenzo that I couldn't see him anymore. I didn't bring up Alex; I just told him that I wasn't comfortable with his lifestyle. The real truth was that I needed to spend some time alone. I needed to look at what was going on with me that I would allow myself to be in one messed up situation after another. The common denominator in all those situations was me, so I must be the problem.

Part Seven:

On Lock

Chapter 26
Love Actually

Julianna's first love, Christopher, moved back into the house next door to Julianna after his mother passed away. He had come back multiple times to cut the hedges down because they kept growing back. Eventually, he salted the earth, and they never grew back again. Christopher and Julianna also agreed to take down the fence between their two yards. When they had parties, they used both yards. They always joked about digging a tunnel to connect the two houses underground so that they could go back and forth without having to go outside.

Christopher cooked almost all his meals on the barbecue grill. Every day when Julianna and David would get home for the evening, David ran next door to grab a hot dog off the grill while Julianna and Christopher discussed their days.

One day, Christopher told Julianna that he proposed to his girlfriend, Alexis, and that he was getting married. He wanted Julianna to be there. Christopher and Alexis had been dating for a long time, so Julianna knew her and thought that she was lovely. She was a good girl. She visited Christopher often, but she was always gone by a decent time of night. And she was very sweet and friendly.

Julianna and Christopher's relationship was complicated. They had been connected since they were children. They loved each other in a way that doesn't have a name. They had history; they had a bond; they had a friendship that was somehow more—not quite romantic, not quite platonic, deeper than friendship, different from every other relationship she had.

Christopher was Julianna's go to person for things that she needed done around the house. If she thought she heard something outside, all she had to do was call Christopher, and he was on his way with his shotgun. Christopher was a painter and he agreed to paint Julianna's garage before David's kindergarten graduation party.

Julianna asked, "Can you paint the garage before the wedding?"

"Why? There is plenty of time before the party."

"Because I don't want it to not get done because your new wife has an issue with you doing something for me."

"Come on Jewels! You know that Alexis is cool."

"I know that girlfriend Alexis is cool. I don't know what wife Alexis will be like."

"It won't be a problem, but I will do it before the wedding."

"Thank you, Christopher!" she said in her softest and sweetest voice.

The day before the wedding, Julianna and Christopher were outside talking and Julianna said, "Are you ready for tomorrow?"

"Yeah, I'm ready!"

"Listen, I am happy for you. I just don't know if I can be there to see it happen; that's a little much to ask."

"Jewels, I understand that! You know that my family is small. I consider everyone who grew up with us as my family. I need for you to be there."

"Okay Christopher, I'll be there for you. I promise!"

The day of the wedding, Julianna saw all of Christopher's friends arriving at his house. She went over to check on them. She knew them all because Christopher's house was the hang out spot. He had the same group of friends since high school, and they were all super close. Not to mention that Christopher had a lot of parties, and they were always around. She walked into the house, and it was a mess—they had stuff everywhere. Julianna asked Christopher when he and Alexis were coming back. He told her that they would be back to the house after the wedding reception. Julianna couldn't let Alexis walk into her new life with the house looking like that, so she cleaned the house. By the time she finished, the guys were all dressed, and the limousine was outside. Julianna walked out with them. She straightened Christopher's tie. He kissed her goodbye and got in the limo. The next time she saw him, he was at the altar waiting for Alexis to enter.

India went to the wedding with Julianna. They sat and watched as Christopher exchanged wedding vows with Alexis.

Christopher asked Julianna to dance at the wedding reception. Luther Vandross sang *So Amazing* as they slow danced together for the last time.

Knowing that Julianna loved and collected seashells, Christopher brought her two big shells back from his honeymoon.

Chapter 27
It's So Hard to Say Goodbye to Yesterday

Stephanie was one of Carmen's friends. When Julianna met her, Stephanie was in the Detroit Police Department Academy. She worked really hard to graduate and was proud to be a police officer. Stephanie was orphaned as a child and was never adopted. Because she always felt unwanted, Stephanie constantly forced her friends to prove that they wanted to be her friends. She would create situations where she was in trouble just to see if her friends would come help her. Julianna liked Stephanie but found it hard to manage the neediness of Stephanie's personality. They talked fairly often, but they didn't hang out too much. In less than six months of being on the force, Stephanie was killed in an off-duty altercation at a gas station.

Julianna thought that Stephanie was a very sweet young lady and was deeply saddened by her death. While she was planning on attending Stephanie's funeral, she realized that Stephanie's being shot down was bringing up all her issues with Craig's death. When he died, Julianna felt as though she had been punished because she had no business dating that type of man, and if she made the wrong choice again, the next person would be taken from her too. The effect was that her fear of being left by men grew immensely. She required constant reassurance.

When Stephanie died in a similar manner to Craig, she began to see that she had not been able to have closure in this area. She didn't see Craig after he died, and she never said goodbye to him. She chose to bury both Stephanie and Craig during Stephanie's funeral.

Whenever a police officer falls, police come from all around to pay their respects. The funeral was held at Greater Grace Temple on Seven Mile and Schaefer. The street was lined with police cars and motorcycles. The parking lot was filled with police officers standing at attention in their dress uniforms with a black strip across their badges. Julianna and Carmen walked through the door of the church, and one of the officers handed them little blue ribbons to pin to their dresses. As they entered the sanctuary, they saw that the church was full of flowers and wall-to-wall people. Julianna heard Yolanda Adams' *Open Up My Heart* playing through the speakers. They walked down the center aisle toward the casket that was draped with a United States flag and had a police officer posted on each side. Stephanie's body was neatly dressed in her police officer uniform.

They sat down and Julianna thought about all the conversations that she had with Stephanie. Tears ran down her face as she thought about how sad it was that Stephanie was only here for a short time but how beautiful it was to see how many people she reached in that time. Her thoughts then turned to Craig and the time they spent together; all the things that happened that had nothing to do with her but changed who she was and how she looked at life. She cried when Craig died but those were tears of pain, fear, and confusion. These tears felt different to her. She was unable to control them. Her body was at the funeral, but she was lost in her own thoughts the whole time. She was letting go; she just talked to Craig in her head until she got everything out that she needed and wanted to say. Her face was soaked from the tears and her chest felt full. In the end, she felt peace. That night, Julianna wrote in her journal.

Letter to Stephanie

I think that you were a beautiful, caring person and I regret that I was unable to be there for you in the way that you required. I viewed your body today, and the first thing that I noticed was how different it looked without you in it. You were funny, silly, and extremely creative with your poetry. It was the part of you that required constant reassurance that people cared for you, that I was unable to deal with. Now, I understand that I couldn't deal with you being that way because I didn't know how to deal with my being that way. I pray that you are finally at peace and that you can see how our whole city is mourning the loss of you. You are most definitely loved. We won't be the same without you.

Stephanie Davis, THANK YOU for being a part of my life!

Letter to Craig

It was twelve years ago that you left me. The day that you died was the worst day of my life. I have been making you wrong for getting killed. I have been really upset at the fact that you allowed yourself to be killed, and at my house and in front of CJ. I lost Autumn after you died too. I haven't seen her in so long. I miss both of you. I want to thank you for staying up all night talking to me the night before you died. That comforted me a lot, but I have still been very angry. Mostly because I made all the things that you did mean something about me. I made it mean that I wasn't enough to make you want to live.

I am 36 years old, and I finally realize that your life and your death were about you, not me. I have spent the last four years not dating anyone, just taking care of my children and evaluating my life and healing from past relationships. I understand now that the love that I looked for from other people was within me all along. If I am perfect, whole, and complete on my own, then I don't require anyone to fix me or make me feel whole. Having someone in my life can only add to my life, not create it. If I don't look within, I will always be without. And today, I am able to say goodbye to you and move on with my life.

Peace & Love Craig Goodwin, Peace & Love

Lisa suggested and Julianna and India agreed that they would all attend T.D. Jakes' Woman, Thou Art Loosed! Conference in Atlanta, Georgia. The speaker who had the most profound effect on Julianna was Prophetess Juanita Bynum. The title of her message was *No More Sheets*. She spoke about deliverance and healing from relationship and sexual struggles. Prophetess Bynum was speaking from her own personal experiences and being so completely honest about her struggle that Julianna related to her immediately. As many times as Julianna had attended church, she had never heard anyone speak in that manner. Julianna knew she liked this lady the moment she admitted to having trouble listening to people who told her that she should be strong and patient while waiting for the right person, when they had someone to go home to every night.

She talked about how every time a woman has sex with a man, the spirit of that man enters that woman. As she was talking Julianna thought about Anthony, Dean,

Alex, and Lorenzo and how she had given herself to each of them. She no longer felt the connection to Dean and never really felt one for Lorenzo but the soul-ties to Anthony and Alex were definitely still there. The Prophetess tied bed sheets around her waist to demonstrate the layers and layers of emotional baggage that people walk around with. Julianna was then conscious of the fact that she still had unresolved emotional trauma related to Dean and Damien.

As the conference went on, tears were uncontrollably running down her face as Julianna realized that outside of the closure she recently reached regarding Craig, she had not dealt with any of her issues with the men in her life. She just suppressed her feelings and went on to the next man. She prayed in agreement as the Prophetess asked God to sever every dead relationship in everyone's lives. Although there were 52,000 people in attendance, Julianna felt like Prophetess Bynum was speaking directly to her.

Julianna was home sitting in front of the fireplace just thinking about all the relationships she had been through. She knew that she needed to release the baggage that she was carrying from her past. Journaling worked for her with Craig, so she chose to try it again. Every day for five days, she spent time thinking about each of the men from her past and wrote in her journal everything that she needed to say to get closure so that she could move on.

Day 1: *Letter to Lorenzo*

I am ashamed to say that I absolutely used you to hurt Alex. My relationship with you turned into my way of not having to deal with him and what happened between us. I saw when you began to have feelings for me. I'm sorry that I was unable to return those feelings. I just didn't have it in me at the time. It sounds terrible but the strongest thing I felt for you was lust. You were always good to me and my children, and I appreciate that more than you'll ever know.

I don't agree with everything that you've done in your life, but despite what I told you, that is not why I stopped seeing you. I stopped seeing you because I just couldn't continue to hurt Alex. I did enjoy our time together, and I wish you nothing but the best in your life.

Goodbye Lorenzo

Day 2: *Letter to Alex*

I am very unhappy with the state of our relationship. I know that it was inappropriate from the beginning. You were supposed to be fun and safe. I was supposed to be able to be with you with no worries. Before I realized it, the wall protecting my heart had fallen down without my permission. I turned around and fell in love with you for real. We did such a great job of blocking out the rest of the world that I began to believe that it didn't exist. I didn't care about Quintella and how our actions would hurt her, and that was wrong.

I never had to deal with you not putting me first. I didn't like it, and I didn't know how to handle it. Lorenzo never meant anything to me. I thought that I needed somebody so that I wouldn't hurt so much when you left. Choosing him was a way for me to ensure that you would hurt as well. Clearly, I could have and should have found a better method of coping with my pain.

I don't regret any of our time together because I do love you, and I cherish our children. We built a good facsimile of a life together, but I can see now that it had no choice but to fail because it was all built on a lie, the lie that you were ever actually mine. You're back at home with your wife, and I no longer blame you for that. It's where you were before we began and where you should remain.

I am thankful that you never let our problems interfere with your relationship with the children. I forgive you for everything that I feel you've done to me, and I hope that one day you will be able to forgive me for the things that I have done to you.

...Until Later Alex

Day 3: *Letter to Damien*

I still can't believe what I went through with you. That whole part of my life feels like a dream... it was complete lunacy. I should have known better than to be so cavalier with spiritual realms. I didn't understand them, and I should have steered clear. I don't know what was more disturbing, Craig's spirit coming to tell me that you were after my soul or the fact that you didn't deny it. What I am sure of is that I had no business messing with you or any of the things that you were into. My naiveté put my soul at risk and got me violated in a way that I'm not sure I'll ever understand. I invited you into my life and damn near lost my life because of it.

I know that you're still watching me, and I used to take your random appearances as a threat but what I can tell you is that I'm no longer afraid of you. Whatever weakness or whatever it was that you saw in me that made you think that you could conquer me is gone.

Goodbye Damien, May we never meet again.

Day 4: *Letter to Dean*

I fell in like with you immediately. Through my years in high school, I grew to love you. My love for you was pure and sweet. The truth is that I never got over the way you shut me out when the Falcons released you. When we got back together, I have to admit that on my part it was more of a reaction to my situation with Anthony. I began to shut down when I broke up with him. Every time you abused me—verbally, physically, I would have a superficial reaction to it. By then, I was so numb and so good at suppressing my feelings that I was able to go through that drama like it was a regular day.

What I want to say to you is that it was not okay for you to put your hands on me. And I didn't believe it when you said you loved me because you tore me down every chance you got with that same mouth. I just don't believe that if you really love someone you can continuously hurt them on purpose.

Our son is the best thing that came out of our relationship. While I wouldn't keep you away from him, I can't say that I'm disappointed that you don't invest too much time with him. It gives me hope that he won't turn out to be like you.

I forgive you for it all, but I should have left you a pleasant memory which is what I will do now.

Goodbye Dean

Day 5: *Letter to Anthony*

Oh my goodness, I can't believe what I have done to us. We have been through so much, all because I didn't forgive you for one thing. Not telling me about your daughter seemed so major at the time. As I looked back to try to figure out why I couldn't forgive you, it finally occurred to me that it was all connected to my molestations. As a small child, I was molested by my babysitter's husband and as a preteen I was molested by my grandmother's husband. It's not like I forgot what happened, I definitely remember. I forgave them both a long time ago, I just didn't realize what it did to me. In both cases, they were people with whom I was supposed to be safe. I trusted them, and they violated that trust. When you didn't tell me about your daughter, I took it as a violation of my trust, and I ran. Lisa tried to tell me, but I just couldn't see it at the time, and it began a spiral of situations where I just detached from my emotions. If I could have forgiven you, we would have gotten married, and we would have been together for the past ten years; my children would be your children.

It's so amazing to me that you never gave up on me, and I can't believe that I basically gave you my blessing to marry someone else when you still preferred to be with me. What I've been searching for all this time, I always had with you. Now I have released all the baggage from all the mess that I've gotten myself into, and I've learned how to be forgiving. Every time I see the promise ring and every year on August 8 when I receive my roses from you, I'm reminded of the love that we shared. And I know that no matter what's going on in my life that Anthony Franklin loves me and wants me. I understood at the time, but I now have an even better understanding of why you had to leave and become the man that you needed to be for you. I have finally evolved into the woman that I need to be. I'm finally ready for you, and it's too late because you're married to someone else.

There's not really much else to say after that. I hope that you're happy. I hope that you're very happy. I know that you'll always be a part of my life, but I guess that I have to say goodbye to what could have been.

Goodbye Anthony

The following day, Julianna was looking through her journal at the letters she had written over the past week. She felt complete with each person. Then she realized that she had forgotten someone… herself. Julianna was feeling like a new person, but she needed to get complete with the little girl inside of her.

Dear Jewels,

I want to begin by saying that I am sorry for what happened to you when you were young. It is truly sad and perverted when adults take advantage of children. What you need to know is that what happened was about what was wrong with them, not you. You didn't do anything wrong. You weren't protected, and you should have been. But it wasn't because the people around you didn't love you; it was because they weren't aware of what was going on. I know that those experiences stole your innocence and changed you. You lost your ability to trust.

I get that it all began with the molestations, but it's all over now. I am also sorry that since then, I have allowed all those additional things to happen to you. I have made some decisions that weren't healthy for you and some that just weren't very smart. You did forgive the people who molested you, but you have still been suffering from it. You don't have to keep reliving that trauma. You no longer need to give yourself to men who are unworthy of you. You don't need to hide because I will protect you from now on. You can trust me. It is time to put the past in the past. I give you permission to move forward into the future and live a carefree, healthy, happy life.

Goodbye Old Me

… Hello New Me!

Chapter 28
Marcus Johnson Promotions

India stopped by Julianna's house for her monthly outing with the children. What that translated into was that India took the children to the movies and out to eat; Julianna got to have some free time, but she always paid for the excursion. A routine that began when India was in college but somehow never changed. When India brought the children home, she and Julianna sat down for a catch-up session. India told Julianna everything that had been going on in her life. Then she told her that she heard that Marcus Johnson was doing a Wedding Edition of his Black and White Party. Marcus Johnson was a party promoter who held some of the biggest events in Detroit. He was one of Dean's friends, and Julianna had worked with him on a few projects back in the day.

"What? Oh, there is no way that a wedding that big is happening in my city, and I'm not doing it."

Julianna picked up the phone and called Marcus to set up an appointment. Marcus told her that his company, Marcus Johnson Promotions, was already in conversation with another planner but because he knew her, he would sit down with her anyway.

Julianna hung up the phone and told India, "Okay, I have the meeting with the party people... let's do this!"

The only information that Julianna had going into the meeting was that there were to be five couples. They were running a contest to determine who the couples would be, and the wedding was to take place in the next four months. Julianna wasn't just meeting with Marcus as she had hoped; she was also meeting with his Board of Directors. Since she didn't know what to expect and since there was already a wedding planner involved,

Julianna knew that she was going to have to come strong.

Before the meeting began, the Chief Operating Officer, Daniel Miles introduced himself and let Julianna know that he wasn't pleased about having to meet with her. The only reason that the meeting was happening was that Marcus insisted. Basically, this was going to be a waste of her time because he was pleased with the wedding planner that was already on board. At the meeting, Julianna gave a brief introduction of who she was and her previous experience. She presented each board member with a wedding binder. The binders contained detailed timelines of the wedding - every proposed detail from beginning to end. Suffice it to say that after that meeting, Marcus, Daniel, or the Board never mentioned that other wedding planner again.

Julianna soon found out what was really going on. She thought that she was going into a situation where there was a large budget, and she would be able to do whatever she wanted. That was so not the case. Vendors were providing the venue; the catering; and wedding bands were all secured. Julianna hadn't envisioned having to put together a wedding with no budget, but she wasn't willing to let another wedding planner have it.

Affairs of the Heart would provide the coordination, of course, the flowers and the decorations. In order to secure all the other necessities, Julianna called on her wedding resources. Now, Marcus Johnson Promotions couldn't provide a budget, but what they could offer was advertising and a massive audience. What Julianna was able to do was offer free advertising in exchange for goods and services. Meanwhile, Julianna was working with Marcus' Vice President to select and notify the couples. They contacted and met with each couple to tell them that they won the free wedding. It was now up to Julianna to make it happen. Julianna attended the party people's board meeting every week to update them on the status of the wedding. There would be four parts in the day to include the wedding, a fashion show, a concert and party. Julianna always reported first but she stayed at the meeting until everything related to the event had been discussed.

Julianna also met with her Affairs of the Heart team. Through the years, the team had grown to ten members. The whole team rarely worked at the same time but because of the size of this wedding, everyone was required.

Julianna told the team, "Since none of the couples know each other and they will not be able to have any of their friends be in the wedding party, I want them to get to know each other so they won't feel as though they are getting married with strangers. I will be inviting them to all the Marcus Johnson Promotion events held between now and the wedding as well as having conference calls with all the couples so that I can get to know them, and they can get to know each other. I will select a look and dress each couple. It's enough that each bride has to see four other brides on her wedding day, I have to make sure that each one of them looks different but still reflects their personality and style. The brides will be blindfolded during their fittings so they will not know how they're going to look until the day of the wedding."

Julianna continued, "India, as usual, you will be my right hand, my overall backup. I still need you to make sure that the ladies are dressed and ready to walk down the aisle on time. Lisa, brilliant floral artist that you are, I need you to design and create a unique floral design for each couple. I'll let you know the overall look I'm going for and you can take it from there. Everyone else, you will be working in your normal roles. We need to make sure that the men are dressed and ready to go on time. Normally, we only have one bride to dress, but because there are five, we need to pay special attention and ensure that every detail of each bride's look is complete and exactly the way I want it. Now, five couples mean a minimum of ten sets of parents, Kay Elle please make sure they all have what they need and that they are where they need to be. Carmen and William, there are going to be a few thousand guests, and I need you to coordinate with security and work with the hostesses and ushers to make sure that the guests are taken care of. Gabi, you are in charge of coordinating all of the vendors. There will be five photographers and five videographers. One of each will be assigned to each couple. There will also be a choir and a DJ. Basically, I need for everyone to do what you always do… just more of it. Marcus has a huge team of people working with him, and he's going to let us use whomever we need to help us get everything done."

After the team meeting was complete, India had some additional questions.

"You've been meeting with them for a while now, so what's really going on, what type of people are they?"

"Okay, well you already know about Marcus; Alyssa Charles is the Vice President; Daniel Miles is the Chief Operating Officer; Justin McKnight is the Head of Security; Joshua Kennedy is a clothing designer and

Trinity Anderson works with the models. You are going to love Joshua, he's one of my favorite people. He is hilarious and keeps everyone laughing. My other favorite person is Justin; he is just one of the most beautiful people whom I have ever had the pleasure of meeting. Everything about him is fabulous inside and out. The first thing I noticed about him was how much attention he pays to his appearance. He is impeccably dressed at all times. Oh my goodness, his voice just makes me want to... Anyway, he has a great voice."

"Alright, so what's going on with you and Justin?" asked India.

"Nothing really. Okay, something is going on, but it's not going to happen while I'm working on this event."

"What does nothing really consist of?"

Julianna laughed and said, "You're not going to let this go, are you?"

"Not at all."

"Okay, okay, okay, I'll tell you. The boardroom is always the same: Marcus at the head of the table on the left side of the room; Alyssa to his left; Daniel to his right; Justin sits next to Alyssa with Trinity next to him; Joshua sits at the other end of the table; I sit next to Daniel directly across from Justin and no one sits in the seat between me and Joshua. A couple of weeks ago, I went into the boardroom and Justin was sitting in the seat between me and Joshua. The meeting went as usual, but when it was time for Justin to give his report, I didn't really hear anything he was saying because I was fascinated by his lips. Girl, I was far gone. So, the meeting ended and everything was back to normal."

"Then last week Trinity and I were in the boardroom early waiting on everyone to arrive. Marcus called, said he was a couple of minutes away and asked Trinity to open the back door so he could get in. Well, Trinity was in the middle of something, so I said I would do it. I stood outside of the boardroom near the back door waiting for Marcus. While I was standing there, Justin came down the hall. He was looking good, suited and booted as usual. He walked up to me, didn't say a word, put his hands around my waist, moved closer and just started kissing me. So, I'm thinking, I just saw Marcus pull up; Alyssa was crossing the street; I wonder if anyone can see us; why is he doing this; I wasn't expecting this but I'm pretty sure I'm liking it; yeah, I'm definitely liking this. Then it was over, and I said, 'Well, hello to you too!' Justin said, 'good evening.' Then he went into the boardroom and took his regular seat."

India was smiling and said, "WHAT!? Oh my goodness, then what happened?"

"Nothing, I opened the door for Alyssa and Marcus, then we went in the boardroom and had the meeting. I have to admit that I was slightly preoccupied, but we handled our business. After the meeting, Justin walked me to my car, as he always did. I asked him, 'What made you think it was okay to just kiss me like that?'

He said, 'Because you wanted me to!'

Now any time before that day two weeks ago, I would have argued that point, but I couldn't say anything because he was right."

Memorial Day Weekend began with all the couples arriving at the Hilton Garden Inn. Julianna planned an evening of pampering. The men were taken to pick up their tuxedos and then met the ladies who had been driven over to the spa where a banquet of light food and champagne was awaiting them. Everyone received manicures, pedicures, and massages. The men also received haircuts and shaves. While the couples were enjoying themselves, crews were at the wedding site setting up the stage, runways, tents and lighting. After the spa, the ladies and the men were separated for the night.

The team was out literally at the crack of dawn to get everything to the wedding site and get it decorated. The parking lot on Franklin and Riopelle across from Magnolia Restaurant was transformed. Walking onto the site there was a gated archway and a sea of white chairs. The aisle had a one-hundred-foot runner and was lined with four-foot white blooming trees. The stage looked giant from far away. Up close, you could see that only the back part was the stage—the front and the sides were actually runways. The stage was tented and had huge flower arrangements on pillars across the back. The bases of the U-shaped runways were also lined with white flower arrangements. The stage was tented on the top with no sides so you could see beyond it. There was a fabulous view of the sky and water as far as the eye could see.

Saturday morning began for the ladies with their returning to the spa to get their hair, eyebrows, eyelashes, and make-up done. When the ladies arrived at the wedding site, one by one they were dressed and presented to the other four brides. After which they were allowed to see themselves. Then Lisa added flowers and bouquets as planned.

Marilyn was first; she seemed to be the coolest and the strongest out of the group. Julianna wanted her to lead; she would be the first bride to go down the aisle. She was wearing a spaghetti strapped sheath gown with an embroidered lace overlay. She had a single layer veil; her flower theme was freesia.

Second down the aisle would be Vanessa. Her dress was a strapless satin ballgown with a faux wrap and a hand beaded bodice and a long train; her flower theme was lily.

Third was Eve and she wore a strapless ballgown with layers of lace bottomed tulle overlays and had a waist decorated with delicate embroidery and beading. She wore a tiara, and her flower was calla lily.

Second to last was Kimberly. She was the baby of the group, and Julianna wanted everything to be completely traditional. Her dress was a classic white ballgown with a fitted detailed bodice and a tulle chapel train. She wore a tiara, a full veil and opera length gloves; her flower was rose.

Last but not least was Gwendolyn. Her gown's fitted bodice was decorated with beaded floral accents. The empire waist opened to a long, pleated skirt of flowing silk chiffon. Her hair was filled with miniature orchids, and they were also draped down her back.

There were photographers everywhere. Gabi even made sure that there were female photographers on the floor where the ladies were being dressed. Lisa brought all of the brides' parents in so that they could see their daughters and take pictures. Julianna met with Pastor Rodney Matthews to give him the marriage license for each couple. The men, who came to the wedding site dressed, were on a separate floor than the ladies. They took pictures and met with Pastor Matthews. Justin and his small army of security ensured that only invited guests were allowed in the area. Models serving as ushers and hostesses ensured all the guests were seated.

The ceremony began with Alyssa Charles welcoming everyone. The crowd went wild as she announced the names of each couple. The choir sang Kurt Carr's *In The Sanctuary* as the parents were escorted in by models. The music changed and a soloist sang *You Are My Everything* as six female models wearing satin strapless white sheath gowns glided down the aisle while dropping multi-colored rose petals down the aisle runner. Pastor Matthews led all the grooms down the aisle. Then one by one each bride was escorted down the aisle by her father. Each of the grooms met their brides and accompanied them up the stairs and onto the runways. There were microphones on stands at each corner and one in the middle of the front runway to signify where each couple should stand. Pastor Matthews led the couples through their vows just before he called for the rings.

Ginuwine's *My Whole Life* played as five sets of male and female models walked down the aisle. Each set of models was assigned to a couple. The male models were carrying the couples' custom fitted wedding bands. The female models collected the bridal bouquets from their brides. Then they all walked behind Pastor Matthews and stood across the back of the stage. All the couples exchanged rings and were pronounced husband and wife. Kurt Carr's *The Presence of The Lord* played as the couples shared their first kisses.

White doves were passed out to each bride and each groom. Collectively, they released the doves. The audience clapped and watched as the ten doves flew away and disappeared into the air.

As the couples were whisked off to take photos at the Detroit Institute of Arts, the party people were preparing for the next phase of the day... the fashion show. Organized by Marcus Johnson Promotions board members, Joshua Kennedy and Trinity Anderson, the fashion show featured top designers from the area showcasing their lines on the same stage where the wedding had been held. It was now evident to the guests that the couples were actually married on a cleverly designed runway. The couples returned as the last designer was being showcased and they were led straight to the runway. The five couples closed the fashion show out and the crowd went wild again as the couples partied down the runway to *Wifey* by Next.

Each couple had their own section inside of Magnolia Restaurant decorated by Lisa to coordinate with their assigned wedding theme. They were each allowed to invite their families for a dinner reception. As each couple walked in, they were led to cut their wedding cake and take pictures with their families. This was the first time all day that the couples were on their own. They enjoyed the food and being able to socialize with their families. In their own time, they all eventually made their way outside to the actual White Party. Thousands of people, all dressed in white, partied until the early hours of the next morning. The couples ended up back at the Hilton Garden Inn to try to get a little rest before they went on their honeymoons provided, of course, by Marcus Johnson Promotions.

Part Eight:

In Love

Chapter 29
Cinco de Mayo

It was the 5ᵗʰ of May and Julianna's 38ᵗʰ birthday. She celebrated in Mexican Town at Mexican Village Restaurant with her nearest and dearest, Lisa, India, Gabi, Kay Elle, Carmen, and William. Julianna had been pretty quiet lately about her life, but they knew that if they got Julianna drinking her frozen strawberry margaritas that they could find out what had really been going on with her. So, after a few rounds and all of them catching up with each other, the attention turned to Julianna.

Carmen said, "How are things with you and Alex?"

The main problem with Carmen asking that question was that Lisa was at the table. Julianna had to quickly decide if she was going to deflect the question, breeze by the answer or just go ahead and tell it. Julianna's family obviously knew about Alex but what they didn't know was that he was married.

Julianna decided to tell it all and after an hour of background information and interrogation from Lisa, Julianna said, "Alex and I have worked through all our animosity. After about six months of not speaking, Alex was dropping off the children, and he told me that we needed to talk.

We sat down and he said, "I told you when we first met that no matter what, we would always be friends. I meant it then and I mean it now, but it's especially important because we have children."

Over the years, he and his wife were able to work through the things that happened between him and me and between them. We definitely still have feelings for each other, but he is committed to his marriage, and I am committed to his happiness. So, we kind of leave it at that.

As for the children... he picks up Lexi, Zander and David from school every day. They enjoy seeing him regularly, especially Lexi—she is such a daddy's girl. He makes sure that they have everything that they need, and he is involved in their school activities. He hasn't quite figured out how to integrate them with his wife so they don't go home with him, but my babies don't seem to notice that anything is wrong. It's all pretty normal to them."

William said, "Have you told them about Lorenzo?"

Lisa said, "Who?"

Julianna said, "You remember Lorenzo... Thug Life."

Lisa laughed because that's what she used to call him and said, "Oh yeah, I remember him."

Julianna went on to say, "I was in the grocery store the day before the Super Bowl with William, I looked up the aisle and saw Lorenzo coming my way. I wasn't sure how I felt about it, but I stopped and waited for him to notice that I was standing there. I was having a conversation with William, and when he realized that I stopped talking, he looked at me and saw that I was looking down the aisle. He turned to see what I was looking at and when he recognized Lorenzo, he just stood back to see what was going to happen."

William said, "If we had been in the snack aisle, I would have opened a bag of popcorn to watch the show."

Everybody laughed.

"When he looked up and noticed that it was me I said, "Lorenzo Black."

He smiled and said, "Julianna Jeffries."

I smiled back and asked him how he was doing. He asked me the same.

He then said, "I loved you; I wanted to marry you, but I was having a hard time pulling away from that street life. I tried to get in touch with you, but you wouldn't return my calls. I used to drive by your house hoping that I would see you outside, but I didn't want to just knock on your door."

"It wasn't personal, not really. I just needed some time to myself. I enjoyed our time together but the way we got together was just wrong on so many levels."

"I understand, I just wanted you to know that I was ready. I got my life together. I work at Ford Motor Company, and I'm a semester away from receiving my master's degree."

Lisa said, "Oh my goodness that is so great. I am so proud of him!"

Julianna said, "I know right, now you can call him Thug Life Reformed!" They all laughed.

"So, we exchanged numbers and hugged. Which, by the way, I had to pull away from because I could tell that if that hug lasted any longer, it would have been on in aisle seven."

"Sidebar... didn't you say that you heard from or about Autumn?" asked Kay Elle.

"I haven't talked to Autumn since around the time that Craig died. There was too much everything with that situation. Our friendship will never recover. I did, however, find out that she is doing well. She left New York and moved to Arizona and went to medical school. Autumn is a doctor."

Kay Elle said, "Okay, so what's going on with Dean?"

"Well, he's coaching for the Miami Dolphins. He's making that money, so he takes care of David financially, but he's more like Uncle Dean. He always takes David out to have fun and buy him things when he does come to town, but he never sends for him. You know, David has always spent time with Dean's family, but Dean is rather sometimey. Fortunately, he has Alex. Alex still treats him like one of his own. Dean had two more sons after David by two different women. I was so surprised by this; it just seemed so out of character for him. He has never married. He says it's because no one ever measured up to me. But I guess I didn't even measure up to me because he never asked me to marry him either. The closest we ever got to being engaged was when he took the engagement ring that Anthony gave me because he didn't want me to have it. He swears he lost it, but I know it's sitting somewhere in a pawn shop. But hey, I'm not going to act like it was all bad. It was good back then; it just hasn't been good since then."

"Since you brought him up; what's the scoop with Anthony? You know he's still my favorite," India asked.

"After I hooked up with Alex and had Lexi and Zander, Anthony asked me if we could get back together. I said no and I never expected to hear from him again. About a month ago, he found me on classmates.com. My roses have continued to come every year. We met nineteen years ago so I should receive thirty-one roses this year. I have to admit that I was excited to actually talk to him. We exchanged numbers online and when he called, I probably would have jumped through the phone if I could have. He sounded so good. He ended up marrying some chick from California, but they split up three years ago. It sounds bad, but I can't say that I was sorry to hear that. The first divorce that I ever thought was good news. I have thought about what happened with us a lot over the years, and I haven't always been sure that I made the right decision. I know he was wrong for not telling me, but I didn't even try to work it out. Anyway, he has three beautiful daughters that he is very devoted to. I like that."

"Anthony is still in the Marine Corps. During his eighteen years, he was Special Forces and served in three wars. He fought in Panama, Honduras and the first Gulf War. He shared something with me that just made me melt. During all three wars, Anthony carried my picture in the band of his helmet. He told me about an occasion where his squad was under heavy enemy fire and his helmet fell off. While everyone was calling for him to follow them, he went back to get the helmet. Then he told me about another very similar situation, but this time the enemy fire was too heavy for him to go back. He had to leave without his helmet and without the picture. He was upset and everyone in his squad knew why. A few days later a Corporal came into the tent his squad was in and asked for him by name."

"When he went to see what the Corporal wanted, the Corporal said, 'Your name was inside. I thought you might like to have this back—it looks like it means a lot to you'."

"He then handed him the helmet with the picture still in it."

Everybody at the table collectively said, "Aaaw!"

"I know, how can anybody ever compete with that? As Marsha Brady would say, 'He's the Dreamiest!' So, we spent quite a bit of time catching up. I told him that I still have the promise ring he gave me all those years ago. And that whenever I have a bride that requires something to borrow to complete the traditional

"Something Old, Something New, Something Borrowed, Something Blue", I always let them borrow that ring. I have always felt as though it was the only symbol of pure love that I had. It's so amazing that after all this time, we are still so completely connected. The biggest problem is that he still lives in California, and I can't move the babies that far away from Alex."

India laughed and said, "Okay, I have one for everybody. I bet she hasn't told you about Mr. Slob Her Down in the Hallway?"

They all said, "Who?"

Julianna said, "His name is Justin, Justin McKnight. You all met him; he's the Head of Security at Marcus Johnson Promotions."

She quickly went back and told them about the story that India was referring to.

"It's been a year since that wedding. After the wedding was complete, I stopped meeting with the party people. I did, however, begin to see Justin socially.

We've been spending time together continually since. I have very purposefully kept him to myself and away from all of you, but I invited him to have a drink with us later tonight so that you all can finally get to know him. So it was my plan all along to talk to you all about him tonight. Thank you very much… India!"

India lifted her glass and said, "No problem, it's what I do!"

Lisa said, "Okay, well before he gets here, finish telling us about him."

"He's my age. He's divorced and has three children; two daughters—Jada, 10, and Mya is 8— and a son, Jacob who is 6. He has shared custody, so he spends a lot of time with them. We waited six months before we spent any time with each other's children, and then another five months before we let them start spending time together. We just didn't want to get the children all emotionally vested in us and each other if we didn't think it was going anywhere."

William said, "So it's going somewhere... where would that be?"

"We will just have to wait and see. Anyway, we have such a great time together. We started out having times when we had to have our serious work conversations, and there were other work conversations that were casual. We can also talk for hours about anything; I think that the most fun part of our relationship is that our personalities are so similar. We like a lot of the same things. We both like to dress up. I very rarely wear casual clothes and he wears them less than I do. Our senses of humor are very much alike. We laugh and joke with each other all the time. We just find the same things and people to be funny. He knows how to make me laugh, and I know how to make him laugh. People, can I just say that Justin is such a sweetheart. But believe me when I tell you that there is no punk in this man. He has that perfect balance of strength and sensitivity. Now y'all know how I am, so sometimes that sensitive thing tests my patience and my love. But it all works out because he is so sweet, and I needed some of that in my life. Our first date was at the restaurant in the Omni River Place."

Carmen said, "Do you mean the Omni Hotel?"

"Yeah, the hotel but it's not how it sounds. I had a meeting there earlier, so we just planned for him to meet me there after the meeting. While we were sitting there talking, he noticed that they had a baby grand piano. He said that he wanted to sing me a song. I was hesitant because y'all know men are always bragging about how they can sing… and can't. We went over to the piano, and I sat next to him on the piano bench, and he began to play and sing for me."

Kay Elle said, "So could he sing?"

"He really could sing. He sang songs for me that he wrote himself. And he played so beautifully that he could have talked me into just about anything right then."

Lisa said, "Girl, no you didn't!" Everybody laughed.

"No, I didn't. We didn't go upstairs. I'm just saying that he played so well that I thought about it. The feelings that I have when I'm with him are so intense. We are definitely drawn to each other. While I have an attraction for him, the thing that keeps it going is when I see in his face that he wants me it makes me want him more and then when he sees that I want him, it makes him want me more. Our energy just feeds off each other. The friendship is so strong that it fuels the passion that we feel for one another. Anyone who spends more than two minutes with us together knows that there is something major happening between us. That's why I had to keep him away from all of you."

Chapter 30
Justin McKnight

Justin…

I am so in love with this woman! Julianna is everything that I've ever wanted in a woman. I love that she is such a lady, all the time. That is the example that I want for my daughters. More than anything, I want the family life that we have spent so much time talking about. I love her children, and yes, I know they have fathers, but now they will have another one.

I want to propose in a way that will be memorable to her. Any conversation we have had around getting married always included the children, so I want to include them from the beginning. I can get them to help me pull off a proposal that she won't forget.

I'm all set with the ring. I got Lisa and India to go ring shopping with me. We went to three stores before we selected a three-carat platinum emerald-cut invisible-pavé diamond engagement ring. It is beautiful; her sisters love it, so I know she will love it too.

Chapter 31
Surprise!

It was June 30, and Julianna was preparing for Justin's 40th birthday. The children spent the night before over Lisa's so that Julianna could get everything just the way she wanted. Julianna was just thinking how much Justin was going to enjoy celebrating his birthday with all the children when her phone rang. It was Marcus Johnson.

"Julianna, there is something that requires your attention. Can you be in my boardroom at noon?"

"Marcus, you're coming to the party tonight, you know that today is Justin's birthday. Can this wait until tomorrow?"

"I remember and I promise it won't take long but it has to be today."

"Sure, Marcus, no problem, do you need me to bring anything?"

"No, just yourself at noon." Then he hung up.

Julianna walked into the boardroom, but Marcus wasn't there. Justin was standing there, and all their children were sitting around the table in order from oldest to youngest. Julianna was confused for a minute, then her mind started racing.

She went into the room and said, "Hey everybody, what are you all doing here? What's going on Justin?"

"Everything will become clear in just a minute, have a seat."

He pulled out her former chair for her.

"We already act and feel like a family, so what we need to know from you is…"

All at once, the children rolled their chairs back away from the table and stood up. They all had signs that they held face down against their legs.

Except David, who pulled out a bouquet of red roses from under the table and handed them to Julianna.

Then Arianna held up her sign with the word, "Julianna".

Jada held up her sign. "W I L L"

Jeffrey held up his sign. "Y O U"

Mya held up her sign. "M A R R Y"

Then Jacob held up his sign. "M E?"

Julianna looked at Justin who had dropped to one knee with a ring in his hand.

Julianna was quiet for a minute. The bouquet of roses made her think of Anthony. Then she felt tears running down her face as Justin slid the ring on her finger.

She took his face in her hands and said, "Absolutely!"

As she leaned in and kissed him, she realized that the children were clapping.

They spent the next year planning the perfect day. Julianna, Lisa, and India made sure that every "i" was dotted and every "t" was crossed.

Chapter 32
I Do! Don't I?

You are cordially invited to

The joining of two families at the marriage of

Julianna Marie Jeffries

and

Justin Gregory McKnight

Saturday, the twenty-eighth day of May

Half past the hour of six in the evening

The Basemore

Bob-lo Island

It was Friday evening, and the wedding party took the ferry from downtown Detroit over to Bob-lo Island where they were meeting Julianna, Lisa and India. Their father took them over earlier that day on his boat. The wedding party drove up to the horseshoe driveway of a crystal white stone and glass building known as The Basemore. Julianna saw the cars pulling up, so she looked for her sisters. She couldn't find India, but she was so excited that she grabbed Lisa and went without her. She ran down and opened the arch top double white with decorative glass doors to welcome them.

Justin hugged and kissed her and said, "Hey, Babe!"

"Hey, Sweetie! Come in everybody, let's get you all settled."

Walking in, they saw white and chrome grand staircases on both sides that led to the second level. Julianna and Lisa directed them through the white marble foyer past a set of white double doors.

She said with a smile, "That's the sanctuary where I'm going to become Mrs. Justin McKnight tomorrow.

The ballrooms are on the second and third floors. Everybody will be staying in the suites upstairs so let's go up in the elevators."

Julianna and Lisa passed out room keys: Arianna and Jeffrey stayed in the suite with Julianna's parents on the fifth floor. David stayed in a suite with Lisa's sons on the fifth floor. Justin's children stayed with Justin's parents on the sixth floor. Julianna, Kay Elle, and Carmen were in an adjoining suite with Lisa, India and Gabi on the fifth floor. Justin and his brothers were in an adjoining suite with Michael and William on the sixth floor. Julianna told everyone that they had two hours to get settled into their rooms before they needed to be downstairs. Julianna returned to her suite to find India on the phone giving someone information on the ferry schedule. They later had rehearsal and then rehearsal dinner.

The remainder of the Affairs of the Heart team showed up first thing Saturday morning, along with the hair stylists and Julianna's favorite make-up artist, Sydni of *Faces by Sydni*. By 4:00 PM the ceremony and reception site were set up exactly the way Julianna had requested. The previously all-white sanctuary was adorned with red roses. There were two massive red rose arrangements sitting on six-foot pillars on the back of the altar. Two smaller red rose arrangements were placed on four-foot pillars next to them. There were red rose bouquets hanging off the end of each pew that was facing the center aisle. The center aisle was blocked so that guests couldn't walk across the carpet of red rose petals. Clear glass hearts were invisibly suspended from the ceiling at various heights. In a way, the sight of them would put you in the mindset of stars in the sky. White candles and red rose petals filled each windowsill.

Julianna hugged her sisters and said, "Thank you both so much, it's perfect! Now I don't even want to see the ballroom, I'm going to wait and let it be a surprise."

Kay Elle was the Director for the day. She was great at following instructions and between Julianna, Lisa, and India, she had plenty of them. Kay Elle cued the string quartet to begin playing and Mrs. Franklin sang as the guests—wearing all white, as requested—arrived. The lights were dim, but the white-on-white interior of the sanctuary was well-lit courtesy of the glow from the 100 shimmering candles.

The ladies were wearing white strapless taffeta ballgowns trimmed with crystal beading, and sequins and carried bouquets of red roses. The men were wearing white Armani tuxedos with white vests, white shirts, and red boutonnières. Carmen and William were the first to enter arm in arm followed by Gabi and Jonathan and the remaining bridesmaids and groomsmen including David. Junior bridesmaids, Arianna and Jada were on both sides of junior groomsman, Jeffrey as they entered. India and Lisa entered just before Jacob carried the wedding rings to the altar. Mya had a basket of long stem red roses, and she passed them out to guests as she went down the aisle.

Justin smiled as he watched all their children participate in the ceremony. He waited for his bride at the altar wearing a black Armani tuxedo with a white shirt, red tie and vest and a fancy white rose boutonnière. As they stood to their feet, the guests were astonished when they saw Julianna enter in a red rose-colored strapless cathedral train ballgown with flowing beadwork down to the dropped waist and rhinestone hearts on the full ruched iridescent satin organza skirt. She was carrying a bouquet of white roses.

Chapter 33
Poetic Justice

The doors to the sanctuary flew open. Delayed by the ferry, the guest hurried so as not to miss the entire ceremony. The noise from the doors caused everyone in attendance to turn around.

"Oh my God, it's Dean," said India.

Everyone froze and just stared as he entered. Each hand pushing open a door, he slowed down as he realized that he was being loud. In those few seconds you could see on the faces of Julianna's family and friends, they thought there was about to be a problem. Julianna could hear Lisa in the background calling for God to give her strength.

Gabi quietly said, "Please, he doesn't have anything to say... he knows he needs to go somewhere and sit down."

Dean walked to the middle of the sanctuary and took a seat. The ushers grabbed the handles of the doors to keep them from slamming shut. Then they held the doors open because they realized that additional people were coming in behind Dean. It was now silent as this fine brother with a golden tan and black wavy hair in a Marine uniform that he was wearing the hell out of, entered the room and headed straight for the altar. Four men, also in Marine uniforms followed him into the sanctuary. The ushers quietly shut the doors as the Marines continued down the aisle in formation.

The wedding guests thought that the entrance of the Marines was a scheduled part of the wedding and were waiting to see what was to happen next. Julianna saw them approaching her, but everything seemed to be going in slow motion for her. Julianna looked over at her sisters.

India, who was smiling so hard it was amazing that the words even made it out of her mouth said, "It's Anthony!"

Julianna whispered, "I know!"

Justin said, "Who is Anthony and what the hell is he doing?"

Julianna never took her eyes off Anthony. She had so many emotions flooding her system that she forgot that Justin was even standing there. Julianna's friends and family all knew her history with Anthony. They had no idea what he was about to do. Worse, they had no idea how Julianna was going to respond. They hoped that maybe he was just late and would sit down like Dean did.

As Anthony approached the altar Justin's brothers stepped toward him but two of the Marines who were with Anthony blocked the brothers' access to him. The other two Marines turned and stood guard facing the guests with their hands crossed behind their backs. It was becoming apparent to the guests that this interruption was not planned as Justin's brothers and the two Marines were getting in each other's faces.

Michael stepped forward and said, "Okay, everybody just wait! I've known Anthony since we were kids, and he would never do anything to hurt Julianna. He certainly wouldn't disrupt her wedding if it wasn't imperative. Just let him say what he needs to say."

Everyone relaxed and backed off enough to hear him out.

Anthony nodded at Michael, looked back at Julianna, and said, "I really apologize to you both for the timing. Julianna, you know I love you. I know that I messed up, but you should have been my wife years ago. Where is the ring? The first one, I know you view it as a symbol of the pure love that you desire. If you're not wearing that ring right now, I will turn around and leave. If you are wearing it, it's proof that you still believe in the true love that you have only shared with me. And I'm going to marry you right now."

At that moment everyone including Justin looked at Julianna as Anthony moved closer to her. Justin immediately lifted her left hand to see that there was no ring and breathed a sigh of relief.

Anthony stepped in front of Justin and said, "I apologize man, no disrespect, but I'm not going to lose her again."

He held up Julianna's right hand and there it was, the ring he had given her almost twenty years ago.

Justin wasn't going to just give up.

He stopped everything and said, "Hold up, the three of us need to talk. Let's go."

Justin led Julianna out of the side door to the room down the hall. Anthony was walking on the other side of her. Michael, Lisa, William, and Carmen all looked at each other and followed them. The four Marines who entered with Anthony stayed facing the guests without movement.

India announced to the guests, "Alright everyone, obviously there are some things that need to be worked out and if everyone would just be patient, I'm sure we will be getting started soon. Jewels and..., well, I'm sure we will be getting started soon."

India tried to cue Mrs. Franklin to sing something but clearly when she agreed to sing at Julianna's wedding, she had no idea that her son was going to show up and stop the wedding. She looked like she was in shock, so Kay Elle cued the quartet to play something as India left to find out what was going on.

Chapter 34
Happily Ever After

Amazingly, even after the delay, there were still guests arriving. Four couples and their children were seated just before Michael, Lisa, William, Carmen, and India re-entered the sanctuary through the side door and took their places at the altar. India thanked the guests for their patience, let them know that they were ready to resume, cued the quartet to change the music and the ushers to open the sanctuary doors. As the doors opened, Julianna entered the room arm in arm with Justin. The guests stood to their feet and the Marines stepped aside as she and Justin made their way down the aisle. Julianna could hear the questions being asked during several little side conversations and she could tell by the looks on some of the guests' faces that play-by-play descriptions were being tweeted out and updated on Facebook.

When Julianna and Justin approached the end of the aisle, they stopped and looked to the right. Anthony entered from the side door. When Anthony reached them, Justin kissed Julianna's hand and placed it in Anthony's hand. The guests gasped as Anthony and Julianna approached the minister. After a brief pause to allow time for Justin and his family and friends to leave, Julianna and Anthony exchanged vows. After which Anthony gave Julianna a kiss filled with all the love they'd waited a lifetime to experience.

Epilogue
My First, My Last, My Everything

Julianna…

By now, you're probably wondering what happened in that room. The easiest way to explain it is that sometime after Justin and I got engaged, India thought that she should notify Anthony. He was out of the country and couldn't get back until that weekend. Her excitement turned to fear once we went into that room because she didn't know what was going to happen. She was certain that I would choose Anthony, but it wasn't supposed to happen during the actual wedding, she expected him the night before.

Anthony put everything on the table. He loved me, he wanted me, and he'd waited through everything and everybody that I went through. He knew that I felt the same way about him, and he said that it was time... and he was right. It was the hardest and easiest decision I've ever had to make. It was hard because Justin did not deserve it. I loved him and his babies and I always will. It's just that no one has ever compared to Anthony in my heart. Once I was purged of all my past pains and heartaches, my heart was healthy, ready to love and able to forgive. I should have worked everything out with Anthony back in the day. Not telling me about his daughter was serious, but it was not worth losing all those years with the love of my life. That's why it was an easy decision. I apologized to Justin, and I will never be able to apologize enough, but I needed and wanted to be with Anthony.

After hearing everything that Anthony and I said, Justin realized that Anthony was really the one for me and said that he loved me and that more than anything he wanted me to be happy.

I told Anthony that I wanted to marry him but that we didn't have a license. I also asked him how he could get married without his family. He pulled out an envelope from his jacket pocket and handed it to me. I opened it and saw that it was a marriage license with our names on it. Foolishly, I asked him how he was able to do that without my identification. The answer, of course, was that India had provided him with everything that he needed. He explained that taking care of that was why he didn't come the day before. He wasn't going to put everyone through this and not marry me that day. Then Anthony reminded me that I invited his mother to sing so she was out there already. The rest of his family, including his daughters, came over on the ferry with him but didn't want to go in unless I said yes. Michael was already here, and his other boys came in with him. That was all he needed.

All I had to do was say yes... so I said, "Yes!"

Justin said that he had one request. He placed his hand on my cheek, looked me in my eyes and told me that I was the most beautiful bride he had ever seen, and he hugged me. Then, as only Justin could do, he demonstrated what a wonderful, classy, loving man he is and asked me if he could escort me down the aisle.